# The Destiny of Dragons

GW00992145

Jeni Joyce

First Published in 2022 by Blossom Spring Publishing
The Destiny of Dragons
Copyright © 2022 Jeni Joyce
ISBN 978-1-7397357-7-7
E: admin@blossomspringpublishing.com
W: www.blossomspringpublishing.com
Published in the United Kingdom. All rights reserved
under International Copyright Law.
Illustrations by Suzanne van Leeuwen.

# Dedication

## To all my family

10 . 06 . 22

To Chris,

Best wishes from

Jeni Joyce or

Jenny Foster .

# Part one

## The Dragon's Quest

# Prologue

## Carlo

Carlo the Arctic Fox was only eight weeks old and he was frightened. He was alone in the frozen wilderness of Greenland. He could see a few hills on the horizon and a few scraps of stubborn green twigs peeped through the snow dunes but for the most part he was surrounded by the colour white.

Carlo heard wolves howling and his tail drooped. Only two days ago he had seen his mother killed by these wolves. Miraculously he had escaped from the hunting group and now he was alone. Carlo had learnt enough from his mother in those few weeks to survive but he desperately wanted company. Last night he had experienced an odd disjointed dream. In that dream he had found a friend but the friend was a very strange creature. Carlo had never seen an animal like that, his life had been very short so far but he had seen birds, caribou, wolves and of course lemmings. The dream animal was not like any of these.

He did not know this but the time had come when his life was going to be altered forever.

Carlo looked up to the sky when he became aware of strange vibrations in the air. He saw a massive creature flapping its wings above him. It certainly was not a bird. He cowered away from it as much as he could. Then something dropped from the sky onto the snow just in front of him. It looked like an egg: it WAS an egg. Carlo knew what eggs were, his mother had taught him that they were good to eat when they were available but he had never seen an egg as gigantic or as colourful as this one. The egg had just missed hitting his magnificent tail. He was very proud of his tail and he was extremely indignant. If the egg had hit his tail then it would have hurt and it would have spoilt the pattern on his fur. Whoosh – thud – slosh. The egg rolled down the icy slope until it hit a rock and then it stopped.

Carlo looked up at the sky again and the creature was still there. It was hovering and seemed to be looking for something. It looked more massive than ever. He was frightened and hid behind a rock. Then the creature disappeared towards the nearby snow covered hills.

Carlo's curiosity overcame his fears and he moved towards this strange egg, his body close to the snow and his tail lying low. From afar he saw the bright green of its outer shell and purple stripes. Now that was most peculiar. As he came closer Carlo saw movement inside the egg. At the same time he heard the distant howling of a wolf and he shuddered remembering how his mother was attacked and killed by a pack of these creatures. Carlo was lonely and he desperately wanted a friend so that he wouldn't be frightened anymore.

# Chapter One

## The Beginning

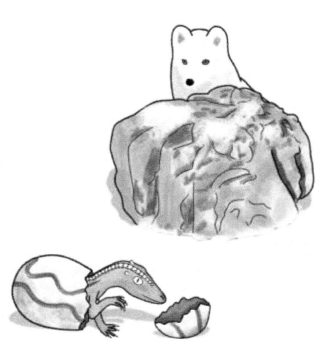

The animal inside the egg had no more room. He was fully grown and he wanted to escape. He lashed out with his legs and using his teeth he managed to tear at a weak spot at one end of the egg. He saw light for the first time and he pushed and wriggled himself into the outside world. First came his claws, then his head, followed by his body and long tail. He tried to stand but slipped on the ice. He tried again and looked in all directions, frantically searching for his mother. He was thinking in the universal animal language and he knew he could speak it as well.

"Where's Mummy? She should be here and telling me who I am and what to do. What's all this white stuff? It's so cold, I don't like it." He looked down and saw the yellow jelly which covered some lovely purple stripes which he saw on his body. He thought they looked stunning. "What's all this slimy stuff? It's covering my stripes, I don't like it at all."

He tried to jump to throw it off but his legs spread sideways and he fell, slip, slash and slosh onto the snow. Then he suddenly stopped trying to jump. He had remembered someone calling out. "Oh no, that egg has gone in a FLASH."

"I know my name now, it must be Flash. But where's Mummy?"

Flash looked back as he heard a menacing growl. It didn't sound very friendly and it scared him. He saw a massive white animal plodding heavily towards him on the snow. She had a black nose and was sniffing the air as she walked. Flash was so tiny compared to this animal. He felt defenseless and wished again that his mummy was with him. Then he noticed her babies.

*Oh, that's good. She looks like a mummy with two babies. I wonder if she's my mummy as well.*

Flash tried to walk towards her but fell over again on the slippery ice. When he tried to stand he caught a glimpse of Carlo the fox hiding behind a rock. Carlo started moving nearer Flash to stop him going so close to the giant creature but then he changed his mind and went back into hiding.

"Hello", said Flash. It came out as a high pitched squeak. The animal hardly heard him. Flash heard a groan from the direction of the rock and he saw Carlo wince as the huge animal lashed out with her enormous paw. When she got closer still she towered over Flash who could smell the stench of her breath.

"What's this?" She growled. "You look stupid with all those colours. I bet you taste nice though. You're just about the right size for a starter before our main dinner. Here cubs, which leg would you like?" There was nothing Flash could do to protect himself, he was so little in comparison to this enormous Polar Bear.

The bear lunged forward ready to bite Flash in half. Flash closed his eyes and waited. Nothing happened and he slowly opened one eye.

He saw a grey cloud materialising and it was getting very close. As he watched, the edges of the cloud started forming a shape. It was the shape of a truly massive bear. The cubs cowered close to their mother who was equally terrified. He heard a soft murmuring that grew louder until it thundered out and was echoed back from the distant hills.

"Do not go near him, leave him for me." Said the gigantic bear shape. "He is just a baby but he has so much undeveloped Power of Fire and Command. I, Nanuk must have that Power but he must be allowed to grow. When he's fully grown I will meet him again."

The Bear and the cloud from which he came slowly vanished. The mother bear and her cubs ran away. Flash was left in shock, lying in the snow. Shaking with fright and struggling to stand he saw the same animal that he had seen before come out from his hiding place. When he came near, Flash peered up at him.

"Hi, I'm Carlo. I saw what happened there and I thought you could use some help. I would love a friend to keep me company." He held out a paw to help Flash stand.

# Chapter Two

## The beginning of a friendship

Flash looked up at his rescuer. "Are you my mummy?"

"Ha ha, no. I'm an Arctic Fox. I have fur and you have scales. I have no idea what you are. I've never seen anything like you before."

Flash shrank away, he didn't know whether to believe his new friend.

"Honestly, you can trust me. I'm not like those Polar Bears. They can be really nasty and bad tempered and you mustn't let them get too close. But I can look after you and I would love a friend." Again he held out a paw. This time Flash grabbed it and pulled himself up onto the ice.

"I don't know what I am either. I think my name is Flash, but I want my mummy and I don't like this jelly stuff. It's covering my lovely stripes." Carlo peered at the still terrified Flash.

"You're strange. You have really sharp teeth and bright yellow eyes. You look like a joke gone wrong. Come on Flash, this way. We'll hang out together and perhaps we'll have an adventure."

Flash did not know what an adventure was but hoped his mummy would be in this adventure. Of course he didn't know what a friend was either. But he thought he had better agree. After all he didn't have his mummy to look after him and this fox would be company.

"OK then, let's be friends and have an adventure." As Flash spoke he wobbled on his feet and he looked down at them.

"I think I had better practice moving on this slippery

stuff before we have this adventure. I can't even balance properly."

Carlo groaned crossly. He knew the wolves were getting closer. He had heard one earlier, howling his nasty wolf song. "Alright, go ahead and practise but don't take too long. There are wolves around and they are really vile and as rotten as bad eggs. While you are practising I will dig for food."

*What's food?* Flash thought. *Why have I got this strange feeling in my tummy?* He started practising walking but then he saw Carlo acting in a most peculiar way. He had reached some soft snow and he was prancing up and down. It looked like some sort of dance. Suddenly he dived under the snow and disappeared. Flash thought he had lost his new friend forever. But then he reappeared with two wriggling furry creatures in his mouth. He raced back to Flash.

"Here you are, here's lunch. One lemming for you and one for me. He threw one to Flash and put the other one in his mouth. Flash looked at Carlo and then at the lemming. It looked rather cute with soft dark brown fur and it was still wriggling. Flash waited until it was not moving at all then he slowly copied Carlo and swallowed the lemming. The strange feeling in his tummy disappeared. "That's better, I don't feel empty anymore."

"Come on Flash, that's enough practising. Let's start walking. We must find a warmer spot to rest before night falls."

Flash had found he could walk much better by spreading out his feet. They started their trek and walked slowly until finally Carlo found a slope with soft snow at the bottom. They laid down on the snow and huddled together for warmth.

6

"See Flash, you wouldn't have managed without me. You should be grateful."

Carlo heard Flash muttering to himself as he dropped off to sleep. "I still haven't found my mummy, I really must find her."

# Chapter Three

## Carlo deceives Flash

Flash was woken by a strange noise and it sounded as if it was coming from the sky.

"What's that noise?" Flash sat up quickly, shaking off some fallen snow. Carlo was already awake and he knew what the sound was. Flash tried to stand but he fell over again. Carlo replied a little too quickly.

"Don't worry about that, we often hear strange sounds. It could have been some wolves howling or one of the human gods prowling around."

"But the noise was definitely up there in the sky," Flash objected.

"Now you're imagining things or you were dreaming. It wasn't anything, I promise. We are both covered by snow and if you're like me you are cold and hungry. I'll dig for food."

Flash didn't reply. Instead, he looked up at the sky, he saw nothing except thick grey clouds. Carlo replied, "oh alright, I may as well tell you. I heard the same sound when you were hatching. It was probably the wind."

Flash realised that Carlo was peering at him very closely. "Stop looking at me like that. I feel like some kind of a freak."

"I'm not imagining this Flash, you've grown in the night. You must be nearly half my size and you've lost the jelly!" Flash looked down at himself.

"My stripes are so clear now. Aren't they beautiful?"

"But you can be seen so easily and that's not good at all. You must remember to keep rolling in the snow so you can hide from wolves and bears."

"Okay, but it's such a pity to hide my stripes. You're right though, I have grown. I didn't know I would grow so quickly. My scales feel really hard as well. I wish I could find my mummy, she would tell me who I am and what to do."

"Stop going on about your mum, you'll find her I'm sure. Right at this moment I will look after you." Carlo scampered off to dig for breakfast. He soon returned with two lemmings. He threw one over to Flash.

"What about that noise I heard? I know it came from the sky."

Carlo sighed with exasperation. "Nah, I told you, that was nothing. What are those bumps on your back? They look odd, I wonder what they are." Flash thought, *Carlo doesn't want me to know about the noise. He's trying to sidetrack me.*

"Come on, let's start walking. We may as well keep going in the same direction."

Flash slowly followed Carlo who bounced along and chattered all the time, mostly boasting about his own bravery.

"I remember the time when three wolves came at me from behind and two appeared ahead. I was really scared and I thought I was done for, but I didn't panic. I stopped and started to dance. I put a lot of energy into that dance and my legs were going up really high. The wolves stopped and watched me for a second. Then you should have seen me kick snow into their eyes. I took the chance and ran. They tried to catch me but I was too fast." He boasted continually about how brave he was.

They walked on and on until even Carlo's stories were drying up. Suddenly Carlo shouted.

"Watch out, there's a wolf ahead and it's huge. We have to get out of here NOW."

Carlo dashed to one side and hid behind a rock. Flash was much slower and was left at the mercy of the wolf who was enormous with a thick, dark grey body and a huge tail. The wolf struck at Flash with his paw and threw him to the ground then he towered over Flash who could see his gaping jaws. The wolf was dribbling from his mouth and his slobber was dripping down onto poor Flash's head. Flash squirmed with terror and tried to wriggle out from between the wolf's legs.

"Well now, what have we here?" snarled the wolf. "I should know who you are but for some reason I can't remember. I know, I'll bite you and I'll remember the taste. Amorok never forgets a taste."

Flash cowered as close to the ground as he could but he could feel anger rising inside him. Tiny as Flash was he could feel his strength growing and suddenly he shouted out.

"I don't want to be bitten or tasted. I want to find my mum and I will find her."

Something inside Flash told him to take a deep breath and breathe it out with as much power as he could give. Ignoring the stink from the wolf, he did this with an unexpected result. A red and orange flame appeared, first of all a small one, then it grew larger and larger until it hit Amorok's belly and the wolf shrieked out in pain.

"I remember now, you're a dragon. I will wait now and find you when you are bigger. Then you will have even more powerful blood." Amorok raced away.

Carlo came out from hiding. "That was awesome. How did you do that? Amorok won't like it, he's the wolf god and doesn't like being beaten." Then he added. "What are dragons?"

Flash had no idea, he was too busy trying to get away to worry about that.

# Chapter Four

## Aarja's advice

Carlo raced ahead leaving Flash trailing behind. The small dragon didn't like that at all so he tried jumping on his two longer back legs. That seemed to speed him up a bit. Carlo looked back and saw what Flash was doing. "Go for it Flash, that's much better."

Flash called out, "I didn't like that adventure. I didn't like that wolf and my mummy wasn't there."

When Flash caught up, Carlo was digging for lemmings. Flash looked around and saw the same boring white colour. Here they were on soft snow but he could see some icy patches and a few low hills in the distance. Suddenly Flash shivered, he heard wolves howling and that made him long for warmth and safety. Carlo noticed this and tried to reassure him in spite of being frightened himself.

"Don't mind those wolves. They're a long way away, we're safe for the moment."

Neither of them noticed a bird flying overhead. She had seen what had happened with Amorok, the Wolf god. She had seen Flash breathe fire and wanted to see him close up.

She landed near them. "Where are you heading?"

Carlo was hungry and in a bad mood. "What's it to you? Mind your own business, go away."

Flash thought this was very rude of Carlo and he ought to explain. "I am trying to find my mum. I have only just hatched and I want her to tell me who I really am. I do think my name is Flash, but I don't know if that's my real name."

The bird replied. "Hello, I'm Aarja and I'm an Arctic Tern. I can see a lot of things up here in the sky. I think you should find the humans. They are strange creatures who walk on two legs. They don't have fur and have to wear skins for warmth. They don't talk like us either, they have their own language."

This was very good news and just what Flash wanted to hear. He jumped up and down with excitement and his tail started moving from side to side. His breath grew warm and a small flame escaped from his mouth. Aarja saw this and thought to herself. *There's no doubt he's a dragon even though he's so small. He will grow quickly and so will his strength and power. I wonder if he is the the one who is foretold in the old stories.*

"How do we find these humans?" Flash asked.

"Keep walking in the same direction and soon you will see three pathways. Take the one on the right. That will take you to a human settlement by the sea. The humans might know how to find your mother, if you can make them understand."

Flash was trembling with excitement. His tail lashed from side to side and hit Carlo on the face.

"Hey, watch that tail of yours. I'm still bigger than you and my tail is much friskier than yours."

But Flash couldn't wait to get started. "Come on Carlo, let's go." He turned to look at Carlo who was slumping on the ground with his tail flat, looking the picture of misery.

"I've heard these roads are dangerous and it's where the human gods are waiting to pounce. My mother told me to keep away from humans as they like to hunt and eat foxes." Carlo looked at Flash silently imploring him not to go on this trek.

Flash didn't take long to make up his mind. "I'm going

to find these humans. You can come if you like, Carlo. You wanted an adventure, we'll probably have lots if you come with me."

Carlo's ears remained flat and he sunk even more into the snow. But he replied, "oh, okay then."

Aarja spoke. "Carlo is right, you'll meet some of the human gods. Most are cruel and want more power over their fellow gods. You won't be able to understand the human language so you will have to learn some of it. That will be a huge problem and how you'll manage that I have no idea."

Flash told Aarja about Nanuk, the Polar Bear god and Amorok, the Wolf god.

She replied. "Yes, I know those two. They are always fighting and they both want total control over all the other gods. There's another one who is a hairless dog. He's horrible and fights the other two all the time. They will stop at nothing to get more power."

The bird flew away. She had seen the baby dragon and she had told him how to find the humans and warned him about the gods he would meet. Now she could do nothing more.

Flash and Carlo started walking. Carlo soon regained his high spirits.

"Well Flash, we've done it now. We're on our way to find the humans. I have never seen any but my mother used to warn me about them. I think they like foxes for their dinner. She said they don't run very fast so I'll be alright." He ran ahead in his usual bouncy manner.

Flash looked at Carlo. He was really fond of the little fox. After all, Carlo had been the first friendly animal that he had seen after he had hatched from his egg.

Carlo didn't race ahead this time but walked with Flash

until, tired out, they collapsed onto a snow bank for the night and nestled together for warmth while they slept.

# Chapter Five

## Flash protects the baby reindeer

Flash woke first and he stamped around to get rid of the snow which had covered him in the night. This woke Carlo and he looked at Flash with wide eyes.

"Are you really still the same Flash? You've grown again. You must be bigger than me. You're beginning to scare me." He edged closer and cautiously put out a paw to touch the dragon. "Your scales are really hard. What's going on?"

"I'm beginning to scare myself. I just want to find my mum and she would tell me what's happening to me"

When Carlo heard this he looked at Flash with resentment. Then with a swipe at the snow with his magnificent tail Carlo dashed off to find breakfast.

Flash started to jump up and down with impatience. When Carlo returned with food he was all set to go.

"Let's eat these while we are walking. I just want to get going."

But Carlo wanted to delay the start. He wanted to eat his breakfast and groom his bushy tail. By now Flash was almost bursting with impatience. He called out, "OK, I'm going now and you can follow."

Carlo decided he should follow Flash who was walking ahead with a newly felt confidence. He was sniffing the air to find any new scents. Flash saw that they were still surrounded by the unchanging snow and ice with a few grey rocks jutting through the white snow. The wind was gaining strength and it seemed to him that it was trying to force them back. The thought of finding his mother gave him determination and he pressed on, battling against it. Flash heard wolves howling ahead and he felt Carlo, who was by now walking close to him, shivering with fear. He smelt again. He had detected something new in the air.

"Have a sniff Carlo. Can you smell anything different?"

Carlo took a deep breath and sniffed. "There's something there, definitely an animal smell and it's getting stronger. I can hear something as well, like thunder."

"What on earth is that? The ground is shaking." Flash had seen something on the horizon. It looked like thick dust and it was getting closer. Then Carlo realised what it was.

"That's a huge herd of Reindeer. I think their real name is Caribou. They could trample us to death in seconds. We must get out of their way."

They dashed to one side and ran as far as possible. Carlo reached safety behind a large rock when the reindeer drew level. Flash was trailing behind and he could smell the scent of fear on the reindeer's breath. They were being hunted by a pack of eight wolves. The wolves were targeting the baby reindeer and Flash could see a young one near him being trailed by two wolves. One was nearly level with it and getting ready to attack. The mother turned round to defend her baby.

Flash didn't stop to think. Something was telling him that he must defend this helpless animal. As before, he felt power rising up inside him and he felt himself getting bigger. He ran closer and towered over the two attacking wolves. The mother and baby took their chance and ran with the herd. Flash was really angry and blew a huge flame over the attacking wolf's head. He dropped dead on the ground and the other wolf howled out a warning to the pack. "There's a dragon here and he has killed Rufus. Run

17

now."

The pack raced away leaving an exhausted Flash and a bewildered Carlo.

"How did you do that? It looked like magic."

"I don't know how I did it but perhaps dragons do that. That's me I suppose."

"How much bigger are you going to grow? That's what I want to know." Flash tried to shrug his shoulders but only managed to look rather silly.

The Reindeer disappeared over the horizon and Flash and Carlo were ready to start walking again. This time Carlo seemed more confident and kept racing ahead and even dancing on the snow. Once when he came back, he inspected Flash's back.

"Those hard things on your back are getting bigger. They could be the beginning of wings. I wish they would grow even quicker and then you could fly and I could go on your back. That would be really cool. I can just imagine what it would be like soaring through the air and looking down at the ground."

"I suppose, but for the moment we just have to keep walking."

They walked on and on. When Carlo returned after one of his jaunts his tail was up in the air looking bushier than ever. His ears were held high and he was bursting with news.

"Guess what, I've discovered three paths quite near here and they're on higher ground. They must be the paths that Aarja told us about. Quick, run a bit faster. I'm really excited now I have found them. We have to take the one on the left, remember that."

"No, Carlo. She said the one on the right. I know she said that. We'll get there and then decide."

Now Flash was even more excited than Carlo. The paths were ahead, they were on the way to find the humans. He tried to walk quicker but still found it hard to keep his balance on the slippery surface. He wished his wings were working, then he would be there much quicker.

Carlo shouted out, "There they are. Can you see them now?"

Flash replied. "Yes, I can. They must be the right ones." They ran towards them until Flash saw them clearly marked out in the snow. "The one on the right is much clearer, I think we should take that one."

"Oh okay, but I still think I'm right. You'll wish you had listened to me when we meet those nasty gods. My mother told me they are really horrible."

They started walking on the path on the right with Flash in the lead. He walked with a purpose and that was to find his mother. Carlo lagged behind with his tail dragging on the ground and his ears low, wanting to be in charge.

# Chapter Six

## The friends discover a snow shelter

"Come on Carlo, stop sulking and hurry up. This is the way. "Have you noticed that it's getting warmer? I like it."

Carlo replied, "But have you also noticed that the wind is blowing more as well? I definitely don't like that."

Flash took no notice of Carlo's grumbles and pressed on ahead with Carlo reluctantly following.

Suddenly Carlo's ears perked up and his tail lashed sideways. "Hey, can you smell something different? Have a good sniff."

Flash stopped and positioning his head to stand up more in the air, took a good sniff. "There's something in the air that wasn't there before. Do you know what it is?"

Carlo swelled up with importance. "I smelt this once before when I was very young and my mother said it was the salt from the 'sea'. I never did discover what she was talking about and what she meant by the 'salt' and 'sea'. Perhaps our adventure will be to find out what the sea is."

"And to find my mother," Flash interrupted Carlo.

After another long trek Carlo commented. "There's a lot more soft snow and not so much ice and it's a lot warmer." This was all very strange and it made Flash walk even faster to find out what else they could discover.

But then there was a sudden change. Flash felt a threatening chill settle on his body. At the same time the sky changed colour to an ominous yellow brown. The wind dropped and both he and Carlo felt unable to move. They became aware of a thick mist looming towards them. As it approached it became even thicker. Now it surrounded them and became a dense fog. They couldn't see each other and both were panic stricken. Differences were forgotten and they reached out to touch one another.

Carlo called out in terror. "Where are you Flash? Let me hold your tail."

With horror in his voice Flash replied. "I am just ahead, find my tail and hold on tightly. Don't let go. We must try to keep walking but we must keep to the path otherwise we will soon be lost."

The fog encircled them completely. It seemed to Flash that something was telling him to go back. Was it possible that this fog was summoned up by one of the human gods about whom he had been warned? That possibility strengthened as the fog seemed to roll over them, hiding everything. There was a sickly smell, a smell that was draining his strength away. Carlo had a tight hold on his tail, so tight that Flash yelled out.

"Carlo, you're hurting my tail, loosen up a bit, will you."

Something was buried in the snow ahead. Flash tripped over and went sprawling onto his belly. *What was that? It seems like a rock but it feels different.* Carlo lost his grip on Flash's tail and he shouted out in panic. "Where are you Flash? Don't leave me, I'm scared."

"It's okay Carlo. There's something buried in the snow and I tripped on it. I'm going round to try to find out what it is. I won't leave you." He had in fact walked into the bottom of a circular wall. He could feel it and realised it was made of blocks of snow. The blocks were joined together. He felt more of them placed above and they seemed to be sloping inwards.

"I can feel an opening here. Follow the sound of my voice and find my tail again and we'll try to go inside."

With a lot of complaining Carlo found Flash's tail and they moved into the snow shelter. Now the fog seemed to be lifting and it wasn't so thick. Inside Flash could see a shelf at one end which seemed to be a resting area. It felt warm and cosy and they were both exhausted.

"Let's stay here for the night and have a rest before we move on. "Flash suggested. He looked around. As he looked back towards the entrance he saw something on the ground, "What' that?" He moved to one side and picked something up. "It looks like meat but it's hard and there's no smell."

Carlo joined him and his tail lashed from side to side. "I know what that is. That's hard because it's frozen. If we could melt it then we could eat it. I'm famished. Breathe some fire and then it would melt. Only a small one though or this snow house might melt as well."

Flash looked at him doubtfully but jumped up and down until a small flame came from his mouth.

"That's just about the right size, blow some more like that." Flash blew some more fire with Carlo keeping an eye on the meat. "That's better, let's see what it's like."

Carlo couldn't wait to eat. Flash cautiously sampled the meat. Delicious, it had a wonderful tasty crispy topping. They gorged themselves and eventually sank down, exhausted on the resting bench.

"Move over Flash, you are taking up too much room. You're growing too much."

"You take up a lot of room yourself for such a little fox. Your tail is too big, it tickles."

Soon both dropped off into a deep sleep.

# Chapter Seven

## Keelut challenges Flash

Flash stirred in his sleep. He was dreaming of a disgusting smell that some animal had given off, he couldn't escape it because his legs wouldn't work. He woke up in a panic and sat up on his haunches. The sky was getting lighter so he guessed it must be nearly dawn.

He heard a scuffling noise outside the snow shelter. The repugnant smell got stronger, it smelt evil. He looked at Carlo who was just waking up and he started gagging from the stench. Flash nudged the fox and gestured him to be quiet. He stood up and edged back to the entrance. He heard an animal muttering to itself.

"Ghrrr, I smell an exciting smell. I bet that dragon who Nanuk saw is in there. He's only little but I must drink his blood to get more power. Then I would be the most powerful god and I could tell the others what to do. Keelut, the most powerful god; that sounds good. Ghrrr, where is he?"

Flash glanced back to see what Carlo was doing. He was cowering at the back of the shelter with his paws covering his face. As Flash watched Carlo peeped out from behind one paw to see what was happening.

Flash looked at the entrance flap and he saw it move and a gigantic paw with thick black hair appeared. The paw was followed by an enormous creature who was the most repulsive animal imaginable. The evil smell came from him. He was completely hairless except for his paws, ears, mouth and the tip of his tail.

The creature saw Flash and stopped in his tracks.

Although Flash had grown he was still not as big as this horrible animal. Flash backed away and Keelut sensed his fear and came closer.

"Helloooo, what a lovely baby dragon you are. Look at those purple stripes on your back. Keelut only wants your blood. Not too much to ask, is it? If it is, it doesn't matter one jot, I will still drink your blood. Are you going to be a good baby dragon and let me bite you? It won't hurt much if you lie still. Or do I have to kill you? I think I've heard that the blood of a dead dragon is more powerful so perhaps I will kill you." Keelut got ready to pounce but then a small movement at the back of the shelter drew the dog's attention. He saw a small white animal with a black nose trying to hide.

"What's this then?" Keelut leapt to the back of the shelter and confronted Carlo who tried unsuccessfully to avoid him. "Oh, another foolish creature travelling by night." He pounced on Carlo who desperately struggled and managed to slip to one side. The bite aimed at Carlo's neck missed and went into his shoulder, he shrieked out in fear and pain.

Flash watched as Carlo cowered down onto the ground and pleaded with the slimy, hairless dog.

"Don't hurt me, don't hurt me please." In response Keelut opened his mouth wider and then closed it again to speak.

"I like it when they plead like this, it makes the killing so much sweeter. This time I won't miss." He opened his mouth again, wider this time to bite into Carlo's neck and Carlo shrieked out again. He shut his eyes and waited hopelessly for the end. But the end didn't happen. Instead Carlo sensed Flash coming nearer. The air around them was behaving very oddly, it seemed to be vibrating with unreleased energy. Suddenly this energy was released and Flash came from behind and loomed over the dog. The energy had been absorbed into Flash and he became enormous.

A massive flame erupted out of Flash's mouth and it was aimed at Keelut's legs. He yelled in pain, Carlo took advantage of the distraction and ran outside.

"Nobody fights me, nobody dares to fight me." Keelut opened his mouth and tried to attack Flash. Again Flash rose on his hind legs and breathed out even more fire. This time the flame hit the dog's tail and belly. Keelut looked at Flash with hatred but this time turned and disappeared through the entrance flap.

Flash shrank back to his normal size. *Where's Carlo?* He rushed outside to find him.

"Carlo, where are you? The ugly dog has gone, you can come back." He heard a whimper and went to investigate. There was the fox, curled up in a hole in the snow.

"I don't like that dog. He was nasty and cruel and slimy." Carlo was whimpering to himself.

"Let's go back and get some rest. We have to walk again soon." Flash suggested.

Carlo whimpered, "I don't want to go back. I want to stay here and sleep."

"I think it would be safer in the shelter. Keelut could easily still be hanging around and you would be helpless."

Carlo reluctantly agreed. "Oh okay then, just for a little while." They returned to the shelter but neither Flash nor Carlo got much sleep.

# Chapter Eight

## Betrayal

Both were relieved when dawn broke. When Carlo woke he saw Flash standing in front of him. He stared at Flash in amazement.

"When are you going to stop growing?" Carlo asked Flash. The baby dragon had grown even more and was now bigger than the fox. Flash could feel that he was growing in strength as well. This puzzled him and he wondered how big he would grow. He again wished his mother was there to guide him. Flash was really eager to start walking but for some reason Carlo was delaying the start.

Flash thought the fox seemed very twitchy and nervous. He was dashing around the shelter and sniffing at each wall and then sitting down and scratching his ear. Then he decided to groom his tail. He looked very distressed.

Suddenly he shouted out," Breakfast, I'm hungry." He rushed outside and a puzzled Flash watched as he did his food dance. There were no lemmings.

"Typical, just because I'm absolutely famished. We will have to look for bear left overs on the way then."

Flash thought, *I'm hungry as well. He's always talking about himself.*

Aloud Flash said, "Come on, forget breakfast."

But Carlo cringed down on all fours as low as he could get and looked appealingly up at Flash as if he was gathering courage to tell Flash something.

"Please don't be angry with me Flash but I must tell you something. You will find out sooner or later." He paused and took a quick look at Flash before he spoke again.

"Remember the morning after you hatched and you woke up covered in snow? You thought you had heard something up in the sky and I told you that you were imagining things. Well, you weren't. There was a huge strange creature up there in the sky looking for something. I saw the same creature looking for you after you had hatched. I think it was your mother. But Flash I wanted you and I still want you, to be my best friend. I felt so alone after losing my mother I didn't want to lose you as well. I have never had a best friend before."

Flash listened with his mouth gaping. He couldn't believe what he was hearing. Carlo looked at Flash, frightened of his reaction and he was right to be scared. The dragon rose up on his hind legs and waved his front claws in the air. He was furious and the anger was rising up inside him. Not only had he missed the opportunity of meeting his mother but he had been betrayed by Carlo as well.

Carlo's instinct of self - preservation took over and the fox darted between Flash's legs and dashed out of the shelter. Flash followed roaring with anger.

"You've been lying to me all this time you miserable fox. You knew the only reason for this trek was to find my mother. You'll pay for this." He saw Carlo cowering on the snow outside and pounced on him. He used his front legs to lift the fox up in front of his face. Carlo trembled and his eyes were huge with fear. He imagined the bolt of flame which surely would come at any moment.

Then a strange thing happened. As Flash looked at the little creature face to face he saw a small defenseless animal in his power. *Carlo had helped him after all. He had taught him how to eat, how to find shelter and kept him company. What was the point of killing him?*

Flash's anger lessened and he set Carlo down on the snow.

"I'm still angry and that's not going away and I can't trust you anymore. I'll carry on by myself so you will have to leave. SO GO." He bellowed out the last two words.

Carlo took one last anguished look at Flash and fled.

# Chapter Nine

## The dragon is alone

Flash felt very alone and vulnerable as he continued by himself. He had felt so sad that Carlo had lied to him. Flash felt it was important to find his mother. On the other hand of course, Carlo had helped him cope in this bleak landscape. He had taught Flash how to feed and avoid wolves and polar bears and also where to sleep in a safe place – well mostly. But Carlo had betrayed Flash's trust and he could not accept that. So Flash plodded on all alone with his head held high, looking forward to finding the humans. He kicked at the loose snow still feeling angry with Carlo. *I'm glad to be rid of that annoying fox. I can't believe he lied to me about seeing my mother. We could have met by now. He said he wanted to be my best friend but that's no way to treat any friend. I will be by myself now so I will ma all the decisions which will be good. But first I must find the humans.*

Flash looked around and sniffed the air. It was definitely getting warmer and he could smell the 'sea salt'. There was more melted ice and more pools of water. But now the wind was getting stronger and Flash did not like this at all.

Flash had the feeling again that someone or something was telling him to go back and not continue the journey. He shouted out, "I am not going back, I am going to find my mother. She will tell me who I really am and why I am here. I am going on, I am, I know I am."

The wind strengthened and Flash was finding it almost impossible to keep going. Although he had grown he was still quite small compared with polar bears or even large wolves. Ahead he saw large flakes of snow that had been gathered together by the wind. They had been compressed into a white cloud that was approaching him. It settled round his legs, face and tail. At last he had to admit defeat and was forced to stop walking. He found it difficult to think but he did realise that he had to find shelter. He went down to a crawling position so he was horizontal with the snow and he managed to crawl forward for a short distance. Then he tripped over a rock and fell forwards, lost balance completely and the next thing he knew was that he had fallen into a deep hollow surrounded by mounds of soft snow.

He was safe and he rested at the bottom of the hollow for what seemed like forever. He had time to think. *Something strange is going on here. First it seemed as if something was trying to force me to go back and now it seems as if someone is trying to protect me. Why is this happening? When I'm fully grown and I can fly I'm going to find out.* Then he thought, *I wonder if Carlo has met this snow and wind. He won't like that one little bit.*

At last the wind eased and after that the snow stopped falling. Now he saw that the hollow was very deep and it was going to be hard to climb out. When he tried, he often lost his grip and he slithered back through the snow. But at last he managed it. He clambered out of his shelter and realised he was very hungry. He hadn't eaten since Carlo had left.

But now he had a major problem, the path had disappeared. The snow which had been blown by the wind had covered all traces of it. *So that's why the wind and snow had come, to stop me following the path. Someone doesn't want me to find the humans.* But for now the first thing to do was to find food. Up to now Carlo had found food using his amazing dance. Obviously Flash couldn't do that. He saw a small pool of melted ice ahead. Without much interest he looked into the depths and saw to his amazement some small creatures swimming just under the surface. *They look as if they could be eaten. I wonder if I could lift one out with my front claw.* Flash found it was not too difficult to catch three of these creatures. He watched them on the snow until they had stopped wriggling. *I wonder if I could breathe some fire onto them and get that lovely charred topping.* Flash jumped up and down a few times and then blew a hot flame onto the fish. *Lovely, even better than the meat we ate in the shelter.* Flash felt proud, he had managed to find food without that pesky fox.

Now Flash had to find the path. He saw some peculiar things jutting out of the snow ahead. He went to investigate. They felt firm to his touch. They seemed to be in a line as if they were growing above something that was buried under the snow. Flash kicked at this snow and underneath he saw the firmer ground of the path he had been following. More success, he had found the path and now he felt cheerful again. Flash's hunger was gone and he could go on his way to find the humans. He sniffed the air and the smell of the sea was even stronger. Now he was really excited. *I'll soon know what this sea is like.*

He had only walked a short distance before he found himself climbing a slight slope. When he reached the top he looked down. He jerked back in amazement at what lay below him. There was a huge expanse of water. It was a grey colour with large blocks of ice floating on the surface. Rough waves were continuously forming and crashing onto the shore. It looked cold and unwelcoming. This was the sea that Carlo's mother had talked about.

Flash rushed forward but came to a sudden halt. There was a steep cliff that came between him and the sea. *How do I climb down this?* The cliff was rocky and treacherous and it would be a very tricky climb to get to the bottom. Flash desperately wanted to reach the shore below. He knew somehow that the answer to his quest lay down there.

# Chapter Ten

## At last Flash meets the humans

Flash trudged along the cliff edge looking for the easiest way down. He was beginning to lose hope when he saw a more gradual slope with some rocks which could act as a foothold. He noticed too that there some flat spaces on that slope. *That looks possible,* he thought to himself. He took a deep breath and started the climb down. Very cautiously at first and then with increasing confidence.

Halfway down his foot slipped and that gave him a fright. The rock he was using as a support was much looser than he had thought. He skidded sideways and when he looked down he was in a different position and there was a much steeper slope. *Oh no, this looks impossible. What do I do now?* He couldn't imagine how he could reach the beach. Then he had a wild idea. *Why not slide down on my bum?* He examined the terrain ahead and he could not see any large obstacles. *I can do this, Carlo would laugh if he could see me.*

Flash squatted down on his haunches and pushed with his forefeet. He started his skid down, but he was not prepared for the sudden increase in speed and he found himself hurtling down the slope to the shore.

At the bottom he came to a sudden halt and fell forwards onto his face. *Ouch that hurt*. He had banged his face on a projecting rock. He slowly hauled himself to his feet and looked around. The sea was very near and it still looked very uninviting. There were huge waves that tumbled onto the shore. When he looked back and saw the cliff, it looked a forbidding dark grey colour. The beach ahead appeared to be extremely rocky and didn't look good for walking.

But then he thought he saw movement in the distance. Narrowing his eyes he could see two dark specks near the sea. And they were definitely coming towards him. As they got nearer he could make out they were animals of a kind, one was smaller than the other. They were now getting even nearer and with a jolt of his heart he realised they were walking on two feet. *Are these the humans?* He crept into hiding behind a rock and watched. Then he realised they had no tail or fur and they were wearing some sort of skin covering. The taller one had longer and lighter hair on its head than the shorter one who had short dark hair. *These must be the humans. I've found them at last.*

The two humans had not seen Flash. They were too engrossed with each other. He could see that the taller one had an arm around the shoulders of the shorter one. The shoulders of the shorter one were shaking and it was making a peculiar noise. Flash saw drops of water running down its face. He could hear they were talking but it seemed like nonsense. Flash was still partially hidden and he was very wary but he thought he would attract their attention and try to get to know them.

"Hello," he called but of course it was in animal language. They heard, turned and when they saw him Flash saw terror on their faces and they yelled out in fright. They fled away from him, shouting out as they ran. *No, they can't do this. They can't escape, I've only just found them.* He saw they were running faster than he could but much slower than Carlo. He ran after them jumping on his back legs as he had learnt. In this way he managed to keep them in sight.

*What's happening now? They've stopped. Why?*

Flash watched. He could just see what was happening. Both humans had stopped and now seemed to be frozen, as still as the nearby rocks. They had joined hands and were looking at the sea and that part of the sea for some reason, had lost its waves and was motionless. They seemed to be spellbound by something in the water.

Flash became aware of a humming noise in the sea. It varied from a high pitched whine to a low drone and it vibrated through the air. It was almost a song but a song full of threat. The song got louder and was now accompanied by a sickly odour that wafted towards Flash and made him retch.

A hand appeared above the water and beckoned to the

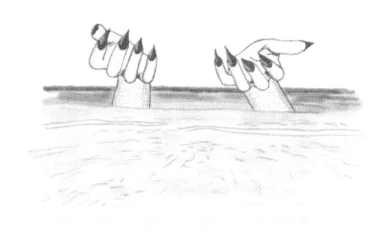

two humans to come nearer. The hand was green with long skinny fingers ending in curved nails or talons that looked cruel and dangerous. The arm above the water was covered in scales, not like Flash's lovely shiny scales but a dirty-yellow green. The hand beckoned again and the two humans started walking into the sea. A green skinned figure appeared above the water with long straggly hair and she extended both arms to welcome them. The mesmerized humans walked even deeper into the sea. She continued her evil song as they walked towards her and now she was laughing triumphantly as they approached.

"Come under the water with me, my lovelies. I will show you the wonders of the deep sea and you will live with me forever."

*No, this cannot be. I cannot allow this. She's horrible and as well as that I have only just met them. I must get to know them and the other humans.*

He lurched forwards and drew level with the creature in the sea. As he moved he concentrated on gathering all his power into his breath. The flame he blew onto the creature was the biggest yet and she screamed out in pain and fury and then looked at him in disbelief.

"A dragon here! This can't be happening. The dragons have gone, they are all dead." She gave out a long hiss of frustration and sank back again under the water.

The two humans were safe but they still looked at Flash, terrified at his appearance. They turned to run away but Flash threw himself under their feet. He sank on all fours, thumped his chest and spoke in animal language. "Me Flash." The two humans looked at him with blank faces and didn't respond so he repeated this. The older one saw what he was trying to say and overcame her fear.

"Me girl, Piujuq."

"The shorter one joined in. "Me boy, Akysha."

Flash looked at them. "You girl, Puja. You boy, Aki. Me dragon, Flash."

Puja then used body and sign language to thank Flash for saving them from the sea creature. Aki started to tug on Puja's arm and said something to her. Puja turned to Flash and indicated that they must go. With dismay Flash watched them walk away. *I can't let them go. I'll follow them. I must meet the rest of the humans.*

He watched until they were almost out of sight and then started walking in the same direction. He could keep up with them as long as they walked and didn't run.

# Chapter Eleven

## The friends meet again

Flash looked down and wondered why his feet looked so far away and then he realised with a shock that his legs had grown. *Wow, I must be about the same size as Aki. No wonder they were scared of me.*

He could see the two young humans ahead; he had managed to catch up a bit. *I must be careful, I don't want them to see me and panic again.* Aki was no longer crying. Instead he seemed to be excited. He kept pointing at things around him as if he was recognising features that he knew. There was nothing there that grabbed Flash's interest. He could only see a pool of water, a hill in the distance, and clumps of the peculiar plants that he had noticed before.

Suddenly Aki yelled out and pointed ahead. Puja had seen something as well and she grabbed Aki's hand in her excitement. Narrowing his eyes Flash peered forward and saw something moving. Eventually he managed to see more clearly and what he saw seemed to be a larger version of Aki.

Puja and Aki rushed ahead and when Flash got closer he saw a strong and muscular human who was carrying a big stick. He had long dark hair and wore animal skin. No tail and no fur. This was a grown up human. He leapt forward to meet the children.

"Where have you been?" he shouted. "Your mother and I have been worried sick. We've been searching everywhere. How dare you do this to us?" He was brandishing his stick as he spoke and his face was red with anger.

He suddenly stopped and stared behind the children. He had seen Flash. He gripped his stick more firmly and let out an ear splitting whistle which alerted two of his friends who had been in the search party. They quickly joined him and they too saw the dragon and raised their sticks in defence.

The father signed to Puja and Aki to move behind him for protection from this fearsome creature. The children started talking to their father but they were speaking together and their father was not listening. He was shouting to the other men and Flash thought he heard the word 'dragon' spoken several times. At least the word was like the animal word for dragon. The men started coming nearer and they wielded their heavy sticks. Flash heard one of them speak to the children's' father and heard the name 'Kiuvuk' used.

*What do I do now? I could easily beat them with my fire but I don't want to hurt them especially the father. I want to make friends so I can find my mother.*

A small white creature with a black nose suddenly darted up to the men and started dancing in front of them. He leapt up and pranced in between their legs, backwards and forwards. The men watched in astonishment and were held up by this distraction. Then they started lashing out with their sticks. *Carlo, he must have followed me. Oh no, he'll get hurt.* But Carlo dashed between their legs and easily escaped.

Carlo ran away and Flash breathed a sigh of relief. The children had managed to get their father's attention at last and Flash saw them pointing to him and making signs. Flash understood that they were explaining how he had saved them. Kiuvuk stared intensely at Flash as if he didn't believe his children. But at last signed to the dragon to come near. Then he said the word 'follow'. He grabbed the children's hands and started walking ahead. Aki was still talking excitedly and Flash thought it was about their adventure.

*I hope we get something to eat soon, I'm ravenous.* Flash had not eaten for ages.

Then he saw something astonishing which took his mind off his hunger. He saw some strange shelters ahead. The children whooped with joy so he understood that this was the human settlement. There were eight of these shelters and they were made of animal skins thrown over a framework of animal bones. These bones were massive and Flash wondered what sort of creature they had used. They were certainly bigger than polar bears. The settlement was full of humans scuttling around on their two legs. *This is weird*, he thought.

They were seen and one human rushed out of her tent and threw her arms around the children, cuddling them to her as if she would never let them go. She kept rubbing her nose to theirs over and over again. She was their mother, Anana. She had long golden hair and blue eyes. Flash saw that Anana was very beautiful.

Then Anana saw Flash and drew back. She pushed the children behind her to protect them but Puja twisted out of her grasp and went over to Flash. She explained again how Flash had saved them from the sea creature. Anana looked very disbelieving so Aki joined in and supported his sister. At last Anana forced herself to approach the dragon and peered into his yellow eyes. Flash dropped onto all fours and gazed back drooling from his mouth. He adored this human and she saw no harm in him. She whispered something in human language and Flash thought that she was thanking him for saving her children.

She turned and started walking back to her tent and indicated that Flash should follow then he heard a sudden commotion behind.

"Hey look, there's our dinner for tomorrow. An Arctic fox is near our tents. What's he doing so near? Get the spears, we'll hunt him." Flash turned and saw Carlo. He must have stayed near to watch what happened. He was twisting this way and that, trying to escape. Carlo managed to get away but the men had their spears now and they followed him.

Without thinking he shouted out "Don't hurt him, he's my friend." The men were too far away to hear. They had their spears now and were following Carlo's footprints. *Why did I say that? I was so angry before but he must still want to be my friend. Why? I don't understand but I really don't want him to be hurt. But I can't do much to help him. I can't run as fast as he can and I think he will escape.*

So he followed Anana to the family tent from which came the most delicious smell ever. His first priority was still to find his mother but he was beginning to realise that friendship was important as well.

Anana had been spit roasting seal meat. She now started slicing it and threw some slices to Flash who quickly gulped it down. Wonderful! The family went inside to eat their portions. Flash stayed outside, his stomach felt full and he was happy now that he had found the humans. Later he heard the hunting men return empty handed and he knew that Carlo was safe. He would rest outside this tent tonight but decided that the next day he would have to learn a few human language words. He would have to make himself understood so that he could ask the humans where to find his mother. Tonight he would sleep.

# Chapter Twelve

## Flash starts learning how to speak human

But in fact he realised that he missed the company of Carlo with his chatter and boasting. He missed the warmth of his body next to him while he slept. He was also worried about speaking and understanding the human language. He was thinking that he would never find his mother. So he tossed and turned all night.

Before the sun rose he could hear the humans moving about, busy doing their jobs. He heard Anana in the tent and he soon smelt the wonderful aroma of meat roasting.

The sun had risen and there was light. Anana drew back the tent flap and when she saw Flash outside her face changed and showed her fear. She was still very wary of him. Nevertheless she tossed some meat slices to him. Puja was watching and Flash heard her voice. The tone told him that she was cross with her mother. Anana turned back into the tent and returned with some more meat slices on a platter.

"Here you are Flash, enjoy it." She used sign language as she spoke and in return Flash sat down and extended his two front legs to her. He then thumped his chest and replied, "Me. Thank you." This was said in animal language.

She seemed to understand and smiled at him. Flash drooled. He still thought she was the most beautiful thing he had set eyes on in his short life. The sky was still glowing with red and orange colours and the sun's rays were beginning to spread across the sky. Men were busy taking large flat vessels down to the sea. They were heavy and the men worked in groups singing as they worked. The songs they sang seemed to fit the beat with the steps they were taking. Flash wanted to know more. He looked at Anana and cocked his head to one side and asked, "Why?"

"The boats are kayaks and the men are going in them to hunt seals. We are warm now but snow and ice are coming soon and we will leave to go inland to build our igloos. We must take meat with us for food and to keep us warm."

As she spoke she used a lot of sign language both with her body and her hands and repeated it several times. Flash did not understand all of it but did realise she was talking about leaving this place. The sound of her talking sounded very rhythmic like the sounds of the songs the men were singing. Flash found it comforting to hear.

*I wonder when they are leaving. I must ask her now if she knows where my mother could be. I hope I can make her understand.*

He decided to speak slowly and try the whole sentence first and then repeat certain words.

Flash sat on his back legs and looked into her face, "I am lost and looking for my mother. Could you tell me where to look for her?"

Anana looked at him blankly and held out her hands. She turned them upwards and at the same time shrugged her shoulders. She hadn't understood.

Flash concentrated on the first part of the sentence. He started wandering around in circles and then in every direction peering at the tent and then at the other humans. Then he tried to tell her it was his mother he was looking for. He pointed to her and then at Puja and Aki who were playing nearby. He then pointed at himself and repeated the word 'where' several times.

At last Anana understood. "Go to the sea," she pointed to the sea when she said this. "Search in the caves, she could be there." Flash understood where the 'sea' was but the word 'caves' was harder to understand. Anana pointed to the tents and circled her hands around to try to show they were large spaces in the cliffs.

When Flash understood that he must go to the sea shore and look for these 'caves', he was so excited that he wanted to go straight away and start his search.

Puja and Aki had been skating on the thicker ice using sharp, thick bones tied onto their shoes. Puja had heard the conversation.

"I, Puja will go as well." She thumped her chest as she said this and pointed to the sea. "I know the caves and will show you." Anana went pale and shuddered when she heard Puja say this. But Puja hugged her mother and then she went to Flash and hugged him. Anana saw how Puja trusted the dragon even though he was so big by now and very fierce looking. She agreed at last that Puja would go with Flash to the shore.

"Come into the tent and I will give you some food and drink for the day." Flash followed but thought to himself, *there's really no need for drink, I can easily melt some ice with my fire. I will show her.* He produced a small flame which melted some nearby ice. Anana drew back in astonishment and thought to herself, *that dragon could easily have harmed us with his power of fire, I think we must trust him.*

Puja and Flash followed her to the tent. Flash had grown so much that he had to wriggle his way through the entrance. He was now bigger than Kiuvuk. As he was wriggling his way in he caught sight of a strange object hanging near the burner. *That looks like one of my teeth.*

Anana saw him staring and flushed red with embarrassment.

Anana tried to explain but her words were too complicated for Flash to understand properly. She pointed at Flash and then opened her mouth to show her teeth and said. "Like you." She circled her arms as she explained. "We keep it for luck." Flash didn't understand that last word and stored it in his mind to find out later. "It is to protect us against our horrible gods." Flash understood the human word for 'gods' by now and he more or less understood the general meaning of what she was saying.

*This is all exciting stuff but when I find my mum she will explain it all.*

Anana then gave them some meat and flat bread which Flash didn't like but Puja did. They left and started walking in the direction of the sea. When they reached the shore Puja explained, using a lot of sign language that the caves were all mainly in one direction. They turned in that direction and started the search. They walked a long way before they reached the first cave. As they got nearer Flash saw movement amongst the rocks. Then he realised it was an animal who was white with a black nose. *Found you*, Flash thought. Aloud he shouted,

"I can see you Carlo. Come here, I'm not going to hurt you. I still think you were wrong to mislead me but I'm not as angry as I was. Come and meet Puja." Wary as always, Carlo kept behind the rock. He didn't trust any human even though she was a child. Flash called again,

"Puja won't hurt you, she's not a hunter. It was the men who hunted you and they didn't understand." Carlo crept out of his hiding place.

"I'm so sorry Flash, I was really selfish and I will tell you everything from now on."

Carlo looked at Flash. "You have grown so much and you are so enormous and those are definitely wings on your back. They look ready to fly. You're scary." Then Carlo looked at Puja, "I'll come but don't you ever dare to get too close to me."

Flash was impatient to look inside this cave. "I'll explain later Carlo but I must look inside this cave now."

"No need for that, I spent the night there, it's empty." All the same Flash wanted to look for himself. They went in and it was, as Carlo had said, empty. Flash was disappointed but he told himself it was only the first cave and there were many more to find and explore. They went out of the cave and sat down on the rocks. Puja opened her bag and found the food. Flash gave some meat to Carlo who was sitting some distance away from Puja, and took some for himself. Flash noticed something around Puja's neck. Aki had worn something similar round his waist.

Flash pointed to it. "What's that?" he asked.

"This amulet," Puja tried to explain, "brings luck." *There is that word again*, Flash thought. Flash looked at the landscape. He saw the cold angry sea pounding onto the rocky shore. There were small areas where a gravelly sand had settled. The sea was grey with blocks of floating ice. Flash didn't realise then that these ice floes would soon get bigger until they had spread over the expanse of water. Back from the shore was the forbidding cliff face and at the bottom of the cliff were fallen rocks and smaller, weathered stones.

Flash spoke to Carlo and explained how he had made friends with Puja's mother and she had told him about the caves and that Flash's mum might be hiding in one of them. Carlo explained how he had followed the dragon after they had argued. He still wanted to be friends and was really sorry about how he had behaved.

They started walking again and found another cave amongst some fallen rocks. Flash noticed the opening first and excitedly, he approached it. Flash got there first and peered inside. It was very dark and it smelt dank and empty. Flash went in and blew a small flame. Nothing! Disappointed, he went outside and they resumed walking. They found three more caves that day with the same result. By this time it was nearly dark and Puja suggested returning to the tents. Reluctantly Flash agreed. Carlo became more and more agitated.

"I'm not going anywhere near those humans, no way. I don't want to be chased. Leave me at the cave where you found me and you can pick me up when you start the search again." Flash saw this was sensible and he and Puja finally returned by themselves.

On their way they passed the hunt and Flash saw the men had caught three animals which he guessed were seals. They saw Puja's father Kiuvuk in a group of three laughing men who were hauling a boat back from the sea onto the shore. They were tugging as one on a rope which was attached to the boat, singing and laughing as they did so.

Kiuvuk saw them and waved. He called something to Puja who waved back and shouted something out,

"I'm okay." That seemed to satisfy Kiuvuk.

Flash made his decision. He would leave to search the other caves on the same day the humans left the settlement. Another thing had been nagging him and this was an overriding urge to try his wings. He felt he should be up in the sky, flying. His wings were ready and there was nothing to stop him flexing them and taking to the air. Tomorrow he would try to use them and he would reach the next stage in achieving his full power.

# Chapter Thirteen

## Flash tries to fly

The humans were on the move very early the next morning and woke Flash. They were preparing to move inland the following day. A group of men were taking their kayaks down to the sea by pulling on the attached ropes. Flash noticed again how their tugs kept time with the rhythmic beats of the songs the men were singing. Flash saw another group preparing the seals caught the previous day. They were skinning them and cutting them up into chunks for transport. When they made the first cut they collected the blood to drink later. The humans knew the blood would give them extra energy.

Flash had noticed the women collecting the roots and other underground parts of certain plants and also the seaweed from the shore. They ground these up together with tree sap to sweeten it. He saw how they kneaded this into flat cakes which they baked on a stone which was heated over a fire. This was their flat bread.

Aki had nothing to do as he was too young for grown up jobs. He sat down beside Flash and started teaching him some human words. He used a lot of sign and body language as he did this. Flash had already picked up the meaning of some words like 'hunt, food, mother, fox, dragon and sea', but now he was eager to learn more.

Aki started by miming the words for 'snow, meat, gods, evil, good, winter', and 'luck'. Then he told him slowly about the snow shelters which each family would use for the long winter. They were called igloos; Flash jumped when he realised that he and Carlo had sheltered in one of these igloos. Aki then explained about the brutal gods who were so much feared but also respected. Aki told Flash about the three gods, Nanuk the polar bear god, Amorok the wolf god and Keelut the hairless dog who all wanted to be chief god and were constantly at war with each other. Qaiupalik was the female sea creature who had almost entrapped the children. She lured disobedient children into the sea and made them her slaves.

Flash asked a question that had puzzled him for a while. "What is on the other side of the sea?" he asked.

"There is a big outside world where humans rule. This is Greenland where we hunt seals and caribou. We used to hunt whales but there are not so many now. They are really enormous creatures. Big ships have come from far away and told us stories of their strange lives. I have heard that in some places it's much warmer than here. I hear Mummy and Daddy talking sometimes and I think they are worried that more big ships will come and upset how we live."

Flash stood and told Aki, "I am off to the beach by myself today, I want to explore." He had decided he would not meet Carlo today. His wings were feeling very big and strong. He had been feeling a strong urge to fly. *Today is the day, I'll test my wings. I will go to the shore and be alone.*

When Flash reached the shore he wanted to avoid Carlo so he turned in the opposite direction from the caves. He wanted to be by himself. There were a few large rocks near the cliff and he climbed onto one. He was trembling with excitement. *This is it, flex your muscles and take a few deep breaths.*

He flapped his wings and was surprised at how big they were. It was the first time he had spread them out. He felt the air pushing against them but nothing happened. He tried again with the same result. *This is not going to be easy*, he thought. He tried jumping and he felt a slight uplift. He tried again and he felt himself rising slightly into the air. Frantically he flapped his wings and actually flew a short distance before he landed with a thump. Success, but only just. He would try again later.

He returned to the tents and found Anana and Puja baking bread. Anana called him over and offered him some leftover meat. Flash gulped it down outside the tent, he was hungry and he knew he was too big to get into the tent. Anana and Puja were talking and Flash moved nearer so that he could hear more clearly. He understood a lot more words now but they were talking quickly and Flash thought he was misunderstanding the words that Puja was saying.

"I want to go with Flash when he leaves to search for his mother. Please let me go. I know the shore and caves and I could help him. I know he would protect me and bring me back to you when he has found her or even if he doesn't." Flash peered through the entrance. Anana had gone very pale.

"I will have to ask your father. You have only seen fourteen summers."

"Please Mummy, please support me when you speak to Daddy. I know I would be safe with Flash."

They had to wait for Kiuvuk to come back but he was back sooner than expected and he was dragging a sobbing Aki with him. He was in a bad mood. He had taken Aki with him expecting him to help with the work but instead he had left to play with some friends who had also got into trouble.

"You stupid thoughtless boy. Will you never learn? You have to help. If you can't work properly then you will have to stay here and bake bread." He shoved Aki into the tent and walked off. Now was not the time to ask.

At last Kiuvuk returned, this time in a better mood. He was hungry and wanted to eat. Anana waited for him to fill his belly and then casually told him about Puja's wish. He reacted like Anana. He turned pale and sat motionless, then to Puja's dismay her father left the table and went outside for a very long time. At last he returned to his waiting family.

"You must know that this is not good news and of course, I don't want her to go. But on the other hand, we must remember she is nearly fifteen. It is time for to have adventures. We must trust her and let her have her way in this. I, in turn trust Flash to look out for her. Let her go."

Puja let out a small scream of excitement and hugged both of her parents. Flash, watching from outside, felt torn. Although he wanted Puja's company he felt he must now be responsible for her and be with her all the time.

The humans were frantically busy preparing for the following day so Flash decided to try his wings again. He went back to the same place and this time found two rocks piled up together. He climbed to the top. This time he flapped his wings before he jumped. It worked, he was airborne and he was flying. This was what he was destined for and he soared higher and higher. He felt power in the air that he had never felt before. The land looked so different and he could see in much more detail, fantastic. He flew round and round in decreasing circles before he lost control and crash landed on the beach. He looked around feeling a little dizzy and suddenly felt tired. Luckily he was not hurt. *OK*, he thought, *time to go back. I've done enough for today.*

He could fly and he was content.

*Now I am ready for tomorrow.*

# Chapter Fourteen

## Puja saves the friends

The humans were up early the following day to make their final preparations for their trek inland. They had to take supplies for the next few days at least so they carefully attached the meat and other food to the sledges. Flash watched and then he saw some animals he had not seen before. Each sledge was attached to four of them. He asked Puja who was nearby and she told him they were 'dogs' and these were 'husky dogs'. They were kept a good way from the settlement because they barked a lot and would disturb the humans at night. Now they were tugging on their harnesses and barking loudly, eager to start their run. The team nearest Flash saw him and snarled. Flash drew back.

Anana had packed food for both Puja and Flash to last them for a few days. When she gave this to Puja she had water on her cheeks and she gave her a big hug and told her to keep safe. Flash wondered about this water and what it meant. It seemed connected to a deep and sad emotion. Of course there were protests from Aki who wanted to go too. He had to be calmed by some sweet meats as a treat.

Flash and Puja started walking before the humans left. There seemed to be no point in hanging around and it seemed better that way. Soon they reached the cave where they had left Carlo. He rushed forward to meet Flash but stopped abruptly when he saw Puja who was walking slightly behind Flash. Carlo's ears flattened and his nose twitched.

"Carlo, don't be scared of Puja. She's not a hunter. It

was the men who hunted you and they didn't understand. She wanted to come to help me and I promised to protect her." Puja interrupted and came closer to Carlo.

"Is that okay Carlo? I won't come if you don't want me to." She talked in sign language and used lots of gestures. Grudgingly Carlo answered in animal language, "Oh alright," but then he added under his breath, *but don't come too close to me.*

Flash took the lead followed closely by Puja; Carlo trailed behind with his tail drooping on the snow. It was going to be a long day. They had to pass the caves they had seen before and then they were in new territory. Puja pointed out another cave but again it was empty. Flash tried to keep optimistic and told himself, *but you knew there was going to be many empty caves, you must keep looking.*

"Come on Carlo, tell us a story." Flash wanted any distraction to keep his spirits up. But Carlo could think of nothing to say, his tail was still low and his ears flat. Puja however started humming a song and the strong rhythm made walking much easier and more pleasant.

But Flash looked around and found the landscape always the same with the flat rocky shore and the black cliff towering over the beach. They found four more caves and they were all empty. They felt tired and bored.

"Let's try one more cave and then find a place to rest for the night. Your mother said there were about thirty caves along here so there is a good chance we will find my mum in one of them."

Puja sung the words this time lifting their spirits. It was a different tune but still a marching song. She had a lovely voice.

At last they found another cave but as they approached

Flash could feel the emptiness of it. *What if my mother had given up on her hatchling and had flown away*. She could have done. Flash shook himself, held his head high and entered the cave. His feelings had been right, it was empty. He sagged down onto all fours with disappointment. Then he thought, *she might have gone round the corner at the back, it looks a big cave. I will have a look*. It was really dark and he had to summon up all his energy to blow a small flame so he could see. It was for nothing, it really was bare and empty. He forced himself to crawl out of the cave to join the others who had waited outside. He didn't have the energy to stand, instead he sat down with Carlo and Puja.

Puja took some meat out of her bag. The smell made Flash realise he was hungry and he ate some food which made him feel a little better. "Okay, I think we should spend a few hours here in this cave. It's a nice big one so we can get some rest."

They went into the cave and Flash blew a flame. Puja surprised him by pulling out a long stick from her bag and lit it from his flame. She placed this in the ground between two rocks to steady it and it gave them light. They chose a place to sleep. Carlo kept well away from Puja.

Flash felt strangely restless and tossed and turned, unable to sleep. He had a weird feeling that something terrible was about to happen. Carlo didn't settle either. Flash could hear him tossing about at the back of the cave.

Flash finally fell asleep as he watched the thin beam of moonlight as it filtered into the cave. But it seemed he was only asleep a short time when he heard a voice at the entrance.

"Ghrr, I smell a dragon, it must be the same small dragon that I have seen already." Flash heard something prowling around outside the cave. Then he heard something else which made him shudder. "I have to swallow his blood, I want all the Power that dragon has got and that's the only way."

And then, someone else had obviously joined him, "You again, you nasty disgusting dog. Go away, I was here first."

"I have as much right as you to be here. It's who gets to him first wins and I can bite deeper than you."

Flash was horrified. He knew who was outside. It was Amorok the giant wolf god and Keelut the disgusting hairless dog. They both wanted his blood to develop more Power to become chief god. They fell into the cave together, fiercely fighting each other. Flash could see that Amorok had bitten Keelut on the leg already.

Flash glanced back, he saw that Puja was still asleep but Carlo was awake cowering behind a rock at the back of the cave. Flash called to him, "Get back and stay with Puja." Flash wanted them both out of the way when the fighting started; he knew he would have to use his fire.

Amorok and Keelut stopped fighting when they saw Flash. Their mouths gaped open, stunned by what they saw. Flash had grown enormously since they had seen him last and he now towered over them both.

"Right, we'll have to work together, whoever gets the first good bite wins," Amorok shouted, "I wonder if the dragon tastes nice and salty."

Flash roared with anger and rose up on his hind legs, flapping his wings. At the same time he blew an enormous flame out of his mouth. The movement of his wings created an air current which was directed onto Amorok's legs. The wolf yelled in pain but then lunged himself forward under Flash's legs. He was joined by Keelut and they both tried to bite Flash's unprotected belly. Flash could not get to the right position to blow his fire onto them.

Suddenly Amorok was hit by a stone and this was followed by another. Both stones hit their targets with ferocious accuracy. Flash glanced back and saw that Puja had made a sling from part of her skirt and she was proving to be an aggressive and accurate sling thrower. Flash saw one stone hit Amorok on the leg and another in the eye, blinding him on one side. Amorok shrieked in fright and pain and bolted from the cave.

Puja turned her attention to Keelut and her stones soon found his face and ears. Flash by now had managed to turn and directed a flame towards his legs which were burnt badly. In the end he too gave up and scrambled out of the cave.

Puja ran to Flash. "That was awesome. How do you blow flames like that? Your wings are working now. You'll soon be flying."

"Your sling shots saved me, you're great with that sling."

"That is something we learn when we are very young. It helps catch birds when we are really hungry."

"Puja, I'm so glad you came with me; that could have had such a different ending if you hadn't been here."

He turned to Carlo who was still cringing at the back of the cave. "Now will you believe that this girl will not harm you? If she really wanted to she could easily have you for dinner with one of her shots. She is your friend." Carlo saw the sense of this and from then on felt much more relaxed when she was near him.

"Perhaps it might be best to try and get some sleep now. It's going to be a long day tomorrow." Carlo tentatively suggested. This time he didn't object to sleeping near Puja.

# Chapter Fifteen

## Flash finds Sedna

Flash was up first. His enthusiasm was back and he was eager to get started.

"Come on you two, it's time to start walking." He walked outside the cave, collected some snow and rolled it into several balls. He stood at the entrance and threw them at his friends. He hit Carlo on the nose. Carlo jumped up,

"You swine, I was having such a lovely dream that I was back with my mother and we were trekking across the snow together. Can't we wait for a bit? I'm still tired. That was an awful night."

Puja reacted differently. She ran outside to join Flash and they had a snowball fight. First it was just the two of them and then they started throwing more snowballs at Carlo.

"OK, we'll start soon I suppose," Carlo grumbled. But let's have some breakfast first. I'll dig for lemmings." Puja was mesmerized by Carlo's snow dancing, she stood absolutely still and watched, fascinated by his graceful movements. When he made his final dive down she started clapping. She wanted to give him a hug when he came back but Carlo wasn't going to get that close and he quickly drew away. He had caught three lemmings which they cooked using Flash's fire.

Puja hummed to herself as they started walking. It was another catchy tune and it made the walking easier. It wasn't until mid - morning that they found two more caves. Both were empty. They rested here, Puja sat on some rocks and they all ate some food and had a drink.

Puja had been thinking things over while she was walking,

"Do you know? I am glad there isn't one evil god to rule the others. We could never cope with that."

Flash replied, "I am worried that Nanuk will return when I am fully grown. That will be soon I think, he won't be easy to beat."

Carlo joined in, "Don't worry about that, concentrate on finding your mum and I'm sure she will help you."

They got up onto their feet and started their search again. They walked for ages before they found another group of caves but like the others, they were all empty.

Flash started to feel a dark despair as if it was a physical being creeping onto his shoulders and taking over his thoughts. He suddenly had no energy and could hardly stand upright. He looked ahead and saw that the cliffs had ended and as far as he could see the landscape was flat and featureless. There were no more caves. Flash was near to breakdown when Carlo asked, "What do we do now?" He looked to Flash for guidance.

Flash made himself concentrate and not let despair take over. "The only thing we can do is turn back. Keep our eyes and ears open and walk closer to the cliff."

They took a moment to rest and eat before starting back. They passed the last group of caves and plodded on. Carlo had regained his usual liveliness and raced ahead and soon Flash and Puja could not see him. They walked round a slight bend in the coast line before they saw the tip of his tail amongst some bushes. His tail was up and they heard him snuffling as he explored.

"What on earth is he doing?" Flash exclaimed. His first thought was that Carlo had caught another small unsuspecting animal. Then they both heard the loud yelp of excitement.

Flash and Puja rushed forward. "What have you found?" Flash exclaimed.

Then he saw it. Carlo had flattened some bushes that were growing near the cliff edge and revealed a short path that led to a cave. The entrance was overhung by leafy branches. Carlo's head was high and his body looked swollen with pride. "Look what I've found."

"Well done Carlo. You have found another cave and it looks a good one." Flash congratulated the fox.

With mounting excitement Flash led the way into the cave. He immediately sensed a difference in the feel of the place. It did not feel dank and cold as had the other caves. Instead he felt a vibrancy which was warm and welcoming. *I can't bear to think this in case it isn't true but I can feel life here.* The cave was too dark to see in detail so Flash gently blew a small flame.

He could now see to the back of the cave and he could make out a large dark body which lay in the corner. With bated breath he crept a bit closer and he saw a bigger version of himself. *It needn't be her. It could be some other dragon.* He was still steeling himself in case it was not his mother. He edged even closer and blew another small flame. She was asleep but he saw faint stripes of red and green on the top part of her body. At last he allowed himself to gasp with joy. This was his mother, he couldn't believe it.

He could hardly speak but he walked back to Carlo and Puja. "This is my mum. At last I have found her." He thought for a bit and then made a decision. "I must speak to her alone. Can you wait outside?" They both understood and left him with his mother.

Flash walked back to the sleeping dragon. Flash gently blew on her face. She opened her eyes and Flash saw recognition appear in them. "You have found me. I've been waiting a long time for you to come. I'm really ill and that's why I dropped your egg too soon. I tried and tried to find your egg but in the end I had to give up."

Flash jumped to his feet and started stamping them up and down. His breath started to get hotter. He could not control his excitement. "Yes, I hatched from that egg and I have travelled a long way to find you. I knew I would find you somehow. I have had so many adventures and I have made friends with a human girl and a fox. Three horrible creatures tried to kill me and drink my blood." With mounting enthusiasm he wanted to tell her everything at once. "I'm so happy now I've found you. Hurry up and get stronger and we can fly away together. But I want to know your name. Please what's your name? Was I right to call myself Flash?"

"Didn't you hear me tell you that I'm very ill? To fly away together would be wonderful but it's not going to happen. I'm too weak and I haven't got much time left to speak. My name is Sedna. But I want to tell you about your father and who you are. You are a wonderful young dragon and full of good power. You must use that power to restore balance in the world between dragons and people. When I realised I was carrying an egg I decided on your name and your real name is Favnir which means Protector of the Weak."

Flash moved to protest but she insisted on continuing. "I must tell you this quickly as there is not much time. There used to be fifty dragons living on top of mountains all over the world. They were very wise and good and kept harmony amongst the humans. The humans you must understand, kept arguing about who lived where, and sometimes there would have been war if it hadn't been for us. For that reason the humans respected us. But one day a dragon was born who wanted more power. He was very cruel and he killed more and more of the other dragons. Mostly the dragons were gentle creatures who didn't defend themselves. Eventually there were more cruel dragons than gentle and the humans learnt to fear us. Now there are not many dragons left and the humans think of us as mythical creatures.

Your father is a very powerful and good dragon. Not many dragons are being hatched now. Whenever one does then we hope that the Chosen One will be with us. I know that you will become as powerful as your father and you also have goodness in you. You will protect those in danger and that is why your name is Favnir. There are old tales which foretell that a dragon will come and restore the old order. As I listened to your adventures you could well be that dragon.

Your powers are growing quickly and that is why you must know the truth. Your father's name is Hogruth and he lives on a mountain which once gave out smoke and fire. This mountain came up from the sea and now is a small island called Vestaris Seamount. It is one of a group of islands between Greenland and Iceland. It's a long way away but soon you must travel there and find your father. He will guide you. Tell him you found me. Look to the sky tonight and you will see me. Now please come close and give me a hug." She said no more; all this was spoken in a very weak voice which Flash found difficult to hear.

Flash held her in silence until she finally died in between his front legs. He had found her but then lost her again and he discovered the nature of the water on Anana's face. He cried tears for the first time. It was a long time before he called for Carlo and Puja. He told them most of what she had said and told them his real name, no longer Flash but Favnir.

Sedna was a little bigger than Flash but she had lost a massive amount of weight because she hadn't eaten. With a lot of pulling and tugging they managed to finally get her out of the cave. There were dark grey clouds in the sky and it felt cheerless. It started to snow and the wind whistled around them. Wolves howled in the distance and Carlo shivered. It took them three hours to bury her under some loose rocks near the cliff face. They built a small cairn over her and then they said 'goodbye' to Favnir's mother under the black cliff.

"Look Flash, Look at the sky." It was dark by now but as Flash obeyed Puja and looked up he saw a bright star falling through the sky. It was brilliant and beautiful. As he kept his gaze on the star, it settled and stayed still and glowed with a piercing intensity that gave him comfort. He turned to the others, "That's my mother up there in the sky. She will always be there for me. That star's name is Sedna."

Favnir knew what he had to do. First he had to return Puja.to her family. He knew something that the others didn't. He could fly. But he would have to practise before he would trust himself to carry Puja. He also knew that he wouldn't be able to carry Carlo as well. He explained this to Carlo who immediately said he would make his own way back. Carlo started off straight away after he had said goodbye to Puja with some relief and Favnir with reluctance. He had the desperate hope that he would see the dragon again soon. He really did want to keep his friend. He braced himself for being alone again.

Favnir practised flying for the next two hours and eventually allowed Puja to climb onto his back. Favnir's quest had ended. He had found his mother but now he knew he must prepare for another quest. He had to find his father.

# Chapter Sixteen

## Carlo discovers himself

Carlo ran quickly for some time before he stopped for a rest near a pool of still water. He leant over it just like Flash had when he was looking for fish. He saw some but they were too deep to catch. He was scared of falling in.

But he did see something very strange. As he was edging back from the water he caught a glimpse of what he thought was another fox. Cautiously he looked again. Yes, there it was but that was impossible. Foxes couldn't be in the water and this one was as handsome as he was.

He put out a paw to try to touch it but the silly fox put his paw out as well. Then an idea dawned. Could that fox possibly be him? He tried wiggling his ears and scratching his nose. Yes, it was him. He didn't understand and didn't trust any of this so he backed off.

The dragon was soaring over the white barren landscape enjoying the power of his wings. Leisurely they moved up and down resisting the pressure of the air and propelling him and his girl passenger forwards. He looked down and saw a white figure standing near a small pool of open water. As he came closer he saw that the figure had a black nose and a long bushy tail and he was gazing up at him.

Favnir dipped one wing in salute and Puja waved.

*Awesome,* Carlo thought with jealousy. *I watched him hatch and grow. That should be me on his back but perhaps he will take me on his next adventure.*

# Part Two

## The Cohort of Dragons

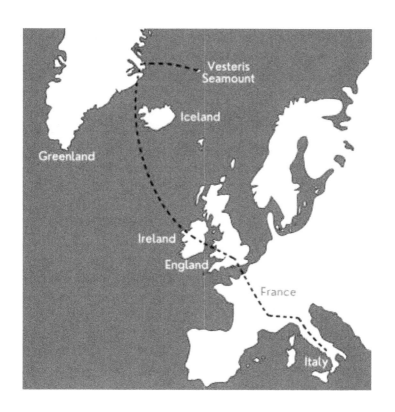

# Chapter Seventeen

## Favnir returns to the humans

The dragon and his human passenger soared across the sky. The dragon's strong wings beat against the air to propel them forward. Favnir could see his shadow on the snow and that assured him that he was indestructible and could overcome any challenges to his power. He knew too that his mother Sedna was guiding him in his quest to find his father.

He heard Puja gasping with wonder as they flew towards her parent's settlement. Before they had left his mother's burial place Puja had practised sitting on Favnir's broad back and she had found a small depression that exactly fitted her bottom. She clung to his scales and felt very safe.

"There Favnir, do you see? There are people on the horizon. I think it's them."

Favnir peered ahead into the distance and saw movement. He called back, "I think you might be right."

The humans saw them, at least they saw the enormous dragon beating his wings on the sky line. As they approached, Puja suddenly yelled out, "There's Mummy and Aki." Favnir saw two figures on the snow waving frantically. Favnir slowed his wing beat down and gradually he reconnected to his shadow and landed on the soft snow. Puja quickly slid off Favnir's back and Anana rushed forward to hug her. By this time Kiuvuk had seen her and he too hurried across. Aki joined in and they formed a group of hugs. Favnir saw tears of joy on Anana's cheeks. This time he understood what they were, tears of emotional gladness and not tears of sorrow.

"You must be hungry," Anana went back to a sledge which they had been unloading. She rummaged around and found some meat and bread for them.

Favnir saw three igloos had already been built and Kiuvuk and some others had been at work building another for himself, Anana and their children. All the humans were interested in Favnir and Puja's adventures and they stopped work for a while to listen to Puja tell her story. When it came to the end and Puja told them that Favnir's mother had died and how they had buried her, Anana put out her hand to stroke Favnir's face in sympathy.

He turned to her and said, "She is in the sky now. She's the brightest star up there and her name is Sedna. I know she's still guiding me. She told me to always look for my shadow. Now I have to find my father. I am no longer Flash. My name is Favnir; it means Protector of the Weak."

"I don't really understand what you are Favnir, but I do know that you are not what we understand by dragons. You are thoughtful, kind and brave and we are really grateful that you took care of Puja." Anana looked into his eyes as she said this and once again Favnir melted under her gaze.

In response he told her that Puja had been very brave when she had defeated the Wolf god and the Hairless dog with her sling shots. She had saved them all on that occasion. He also told her about Carlo and how he had found his mother's cave. He was sad that he possibly wouldn't ever see him again. He looked very miserable when he said this.

"I think you might see him again," Anana told him. "Never give up hope."

Favnir suddenly yawned. He was very tired. Puja yawned too. "Yawning is catching," she exclaimed, "I feel really tired as well." Anana saw and heard. She gave them some animal skins which they could use for cover and then led the way to a hollow near their igloo and told them to get some sleep.

Favnir's last thought before he drifted off was, *I'll stay here for a few days and then start my journey but this time I will not take Puja. It would be much too dangerous.*

# Chapter Eighteen

## Favnir meets Carlo again

Favnir was having a bad dream. He thrashed around in his sleep throwing his great body up and down. He was dreaming that Puja had been captured by two dragons who wanted to hurt her. They had taken her into a dark cave and Favnir watched and could do nothing. In his dream Favnir couldn't move. He had to stand and watch.

Suddenly he woke and realised with enormous relief that it was only a dream. But he realised that it could come true if he took Puja. He looked at her, still asleep. She looked so innocent and vulnerable. He resolved again not to take her on this adventure. *I've a feeling that this time it's going to be even more risky. When I meet my father he will probably be near other dragons and I can't guarantee that they will be friendly to humans. As well as that who knows what dangers I will meet on the way.*

Puja stirred in her sleep and rubbed her eyes. She looked at Favnir, "Thank you for bringing me home safely. Please say that you will be my friend forever and ever."

"Of course I will Puja. You will always be very special to me. But you must know that you can't come with me to find my father. It will be much too dangerous and of course your parents would never allow it. The journey is a lot longer and I will have to cross the sea to another country."

Puja nodded but tears were pouring down her face. Favnir continued, "I'll stay here for a few days before I go. But I will come back, I promise you that."

Favnir saw Anana coming over to them with their breakfast. When they had eaten Favnir said, "I'm sure that your family would like time with you alone for a few hours. I'll go off by myself for a bit and make sure we will have time together later. Don't worry about me, I'll be fine."

Favnir decided to follow a half circular route away from and around the settlement. Not too far and if he got lost he could always fly and get a map's view. He already knew that the terrain didn't vary much. Snow and ice were everywhere. The humans had chosen a small valley surrounded by gentle hills. There were a few small bushes peeping through the snow and some scattered rocks. They were usually dark grey with some green growth on top. There wasn't much to explore but he wanted to be by himself for a little while just to think.

That wish was fulfilled for an hour but then he noticed a swift movement in between some rocks ahead of him. He looked again and saw half of a magnificent white tail with a black tip. *Was it? Could it be?* He got closer and he saw a face peeping out from the rock cover. With joy he recognised his friend.

"Carlo," he shouted. He had really missed the little fox. Carlo came out from hiding. As always he was being cautious. He didn't really know if Favnir wanted to see him. "How did you find me?"

"Oh, I followed the direction that you took when you were flying and I kept on walking while you slept, I didn't get much sleep but I knew I would find you in the end. I saw the human settlement and kept away from them of course. But it was easy. Can I be your friend again Flash?"

"Carlo, I'm so pleased to see you. Of course we are friends but I'm going to find my father soon and it will be very dangerous. Keep with me for now and it will be like old times. But I'm not Flash anymore, I'm Favnir. You must call me by that name."

"That's a horrible long name. It doesn't sound right. I'll still call you Flash. I'm used to that.

Favnir chuckled. He had thought the fox would react like this.

"Okay, you can call me Flash." Inside he thought, *with Carlo I will be Flash but I will keep to Favnir otherwise. After all that is the name that my mother gave me.*

"Let's walk together for a bit. I'm not going back to the human camp though, that's just not going to happen." So they followed the course that Favnir was taking. It wasn't long before Carlo was boasting as always about his skills.

"Must tell you this Flash. Yesterday when I had almost found you, I saw Amorok. He was skulking and sniffing the ground just in front of me. I made sure he didn't see me of course. He went round and round sniff, sniff, in circles. I hid behind a rock and in the end he seemed to give up and walked away. I must admit I was a bit scared. He's so huge and fierce. But I was okay."

Favnir was worried when he heard this. "I think he was trying to track me by my scent. But I was in the air flying so he couldn't find anything. I hope he's not nearby. He might find me now I'm on the ground as I have left my scent around. Let's hurry back to the settlement."

"You can go back, I'll keep close but out of the way of the humans." So they continued their circular tour back to find Puja and her family. When they saw the igloos Favnir went on by himself.

"Guess what? Favnir couldn't wait to tell Puja. "I met Carlo out there. He had followed my trail. But he still calls me Flash."

"Oh, I'm really glad Carlo's turned up, I thought he wouldn't want to change your name. I suppose then we must be careful about using your name when he's around."

That evening Favvo was introduced to a social gathering. They all met outside the igloos which were now built, including Puja's. They built a fire outside in the centre of some rocks and placed joints of meat onto a rack which they placed over the fire. Two of them played melodies on a string instrument and two blew down tubes to produce pleasant sounds. One had a drum kit which he banged in time with the rhythm. Then they all joined together and sung in tune to the music.

Favnir found it fascinating and somehow comforting. Puja was sitting near him but he was watching Anana who was singing a solo. He was again awestruck by her beauty and her lovely singing voice.

When the fire embers were dying down Favnir settled near it for sleep. Puja called to him as she disappeared into her igloo. "Have a good night's sleep Favnir."

# Chapter Nineteen

## Nanuk challenges Favnir again

When Favnir woke he stood and stretched his muscles then he looked down at himself and realised he was still growing. He hadn't yet reached his full size. His instinct was to make sure he was fully adult before he met his father. He thought he would keep his promise to see Carlo and go exploring again, this time a bit further away from the settlement. He would risk meeting with Amorok. After all he could fly now and escape easily. Anana brought him breakfast and when he had eaten, he called to Puja and told her he was leaving for a little while to become more used to his surroundings. He promised to spend time with her when he returned.

Anana gave him some food which he tucked under one of his back scales and off he went, feeling happy and confident. Very soon a familiar white animal with a black nose jumped in front of him.

"Boo, I bet I made you jump," Carlo cried. Favnir had been thinking deeply so the fox did surprise him but he was really happy to see him.

"I'm going exploring today. Are you coming with me?"

"You bet I am. Lead the way. You need someone to look out for you". Carlo laughed.

Once again the two walked together just as they had done before. Favnir made sure he passed his scent onto nearby bushes and rocks as they ambled along. Nothing happened for a long time and it was really enjoyable as Favnir listened to Carlo telling his stories which Favnir now knew were mostly made up by the fox.

Then in the middle of one tale Favnir noticed that a dark grey mist was gathering in front of them and blocking their way. He also noticed that his shadow had disappeared. Carlo didn't see the mist at first but when it got thicker he was worried about what it meant. The mist soon surrounded them.

"Does this remind you of something Flash?" It's just like when we got lost before in that awful fog and we found the igloo."

"Yes, I remember that day. I had a feeling then that someone was trying to stop me finding my mother and they made the fog. I'm wondering ......." His voice tailed off as he noticed the edges of the fog were beginning to make a certain pattern. The pattern then set itself into the outlines of a gigantic animal and that animal was a bear. Nanuk had returned.

Favnir's legs collapsed under him as he gazed terror stricken at the Polar Bear God. He was vaguely aware that Carlo had hidden behind a rock. Favnir seemed to have lost the power of speech. Nanuk's voice boomed out and made the snow shake.

"So we meet again, Favnir. I have been following your exploits and I know your real name. Even now you have not reached your full size and are not aware of your full power. So I will wait until you have. You are no use to me until you are fully grown. You are leaving soon to find your father and that will be very dangerous. I don't want you to be killed before I have gained your power. I am telling you now that you must find the Glittering Stone. That will protect you. Look for it in a deep gorge."

The fog cleared and Nanuk dissolved away but Favnir still heard his menacing growls and he just made out the words, "Until we meet again, you pint sized dragon."

Carlo crept out of his hiding place and came across to Favnir. He put out a consoling paw and touched Favnir's face. "Cheer up Flash. You can beat him. When you are fully grown you will have your full power and I know you will win."

"He's so terribly powerful, Carlo. I can't help being frightened. But I suppose you're right and when I have reached my full size then I will at least put up a good fight."

"That's the dragon I know. Come on, let's go back. Perhaps you could fly and I could ride on your back?"

That made Favnir smile. He knew that was what Carlo had been planning for ages. But he thought it was probably a good idea. "Okay, climb on and try to find the place where Puja sat."

It wasn't long before they were in the air. Favnir had no more use for his scent as he could see for miles around and he soon spotted the settlement. Carlo sat on his back and yelped with excitement as the dragon beat his great wings. The fox loved it.

Favnir knew Carlo didn't want to go near the humans so he landed a little way away and Carlo climbed down. "That was the greatest thing ever. Thanks Flash."

Favnir walked over to the igloos alone.

# Chapter Twenty

## Favnir learns about maps

Seeing Nanuk had really alarmed Favnir. It had reawakened memories of when he had just hatched and Nanuk had come to look at him. He knew he would have to grow some more before he left the settlement. Also he was scared of meeting Amorok and decided not to go so far from the igloos in future. But he would need to see Carlo to explain that he wasn't ignoring him.

He joined the humans that evening. No party tonight but instead he joined his 'family' as he was beginning to call them and ate the food that Anana had prepared. Puja and Aki both had a friend with them this time and they laughed and chattered together.

Favnir wanted to find out how to find his father's mountain and roughly how far he would have to fly. He decided to ask Kiuvuk. Favnir made sure he was squatting near him and during a break in the chatter he asked him. "Do you know where to find a place called Vestaris Seamount? That's where my father is living with some other dragons. My mother told me before she died that I should go there to find him. It sounds as if it should be in the sea. Perhaps it is an island?"

Kiuvuk turned and looked at Favnir for a long time before he replied. "I have never been there myself but I have met someone from one of the boats who had travelled from a country called Iceland. I think he said that he went past a peculiar shaped island on his way to Greenland and I'm sure he mentioned that name. It was probably once under the sea and a volcano erupted and came up above the water. If it is that one then you must travel north to the top of Greenland and then fly across the sea towards Iceland. It's a very long way though and you must be careful. The sea is very cold and rough and you must make sure you are strong enough to fly that far."

Anana had heard this and went inside the igloo. She seemed to be looking for something and when she returned she was carrying a parchment which she spread out on a rug. The parchment looked old and frail and there were lines and pictures on it. "This is an old map of Greenland and it shows the Greenland Sea where you will find the Vestaris Seamount. One of the humans who came to visit us on one of the big ships showed it to me and then left it behind by mistake."

Favnir poured over the map and saw a jumble of lines and symbols. He couldn't make sense of it. Anana tried to explain, "Try to imagine you are flying over the land. This map shows the outline of what you would see from the air. The blue colour is the sea, the dark brown are the mountains and the white colour is the ice."

Favnir understood most of what she was saying, "This could be useful, I could use this to find my way."

Anana looked at Kiuvuk with a questioning look on her face. He nodded and Anana said, "Take it with you Favnir. Use it well and promise me that you will give it back to us when you return."

"Ohhhh, do you really mean that? That would be really great."

Favnir thought that he would use the rest of that day and the next to get to know how to use the map. He would have to work out distances and how long it would take him to fly to Vestaris.

# Chapter Twenty-One

## Aarja's gift to Favnir

It was two days before he saw Carlo again. By then he had understood how to use the map and knew he would have to fly about 700 miles north and then about 200 miles across the Greenland Sea to find Vestaris Seamount. That meant about two days flight travelling at the speed of 45 mph. to get to a place called Sydkap. Each day he would have to fly for about seven hours. It would be a long and dangerous flight with very few rests. Favvo also was worried about being seen by humans. That must not happen. He was doing a lot of thinking as he was walking a short distance away from the settlement.

Carlo crept out from behind a rock, "If I didn't know you, I would be terrified," he exclaimed. "You are so enormous and frightening. I can still see your stripes though. That proves to me that you are still 'Flash'."

Favnir felt different. He knew he had almost reached his full size and he spread his wings and blew some fire to show Carlo his strength. "Yes, Carlo, I'm ready. Tomorrow I will leave to find my father. I know it will be dangerous but I must know my full story."

"Okay then. Let's have an amazing flight today. Go on, let me climb onto your back again and we'll soar up and over those low clouds and see everything from the air."

Favvo thought, *there's no harm in that I suppose*. Aloud he said, "Alright, climb on. That will help me to see things from the air." He told Carlo about the map that Anana had given him. Then he said. "Don't forget, you're not coming with me Carlo. I have to find my own way this time.

You're not really very brave are you?"

Cheeky as always, Carlo answered, "I'm not brave but I know better than you how to avoid dangerous situations. I just run away."

Carlo found the place where he had sat before and clung on as the dragon soared up into the air. Carlo shrieked with delight as they reached the first low clouds and saw the ground as the birds saw it every day. It was the highest that Favvo had flown and even though he could see his shadow on the ground it was very tiny. He saw the small hills in the distance and the struggling shrubs, he saw water pools which were now ice. He saw the settlement of igloos, now eight of them and he saw the humans doing their daily jobs. He realised that what he was looking at was a map of the whole area. At the moment he was flying south of the settlement but he would have to travel north where he had been told it would be even colder.

He was flying slowly as he didn't want Carlo to fall but now he shouted out, "Hold on tight Carlo, I'm going to fly faster." He swung his great wings forward and then back at increased speed and accelerated. Carlo very nearly fell but hung on for dear life. No longer time to look at the ground, instead he screamed with fright. Favnir kept at this speed for a few minutes then he slowed down and Carlo let out a great sigh of relief.

Favnir landed soon after and said, "Now you silly fox, do you see why you can't come?" Carlo was trembling on the ice.

"I still want to come. Now I know what to expect I can cope. If I had a harness of some sort it would be fine."

"I'll think about it." Favnir was relenting, after all it would be wonderful to have company.

A small bird landed on the ice near them. "Hiya," she

said.

Carlo groaned, "It's Aarja again. Don't tell us to go on another dangerous journey please."

Favnir said, "Hello Aarja, what's the news this time? As you probably know I found my mother, Sedna who is now in the sky. I have grown so I am no longer Flash but I have another name, Favnir."

"Yes, I do know all that, I've been keeping track with all that you've been up to. I must say you have done so much and now you are almost fully grown. I had my doubts when we last met but you've turned up trumps. Even you Carlo." The bird turned to the fox and dipped her head in a bow. Carlo swelled up with pride. *Perhaps she wasn't so bad after all.*

"But," Aarja continued. "You are going on an even more dangerous journey. Find Nanuk's glittery stone that will protect you. But remember how dangerous Nanuk is; he is the most powerful of all the human gods and he wants your full grown power. If he gets that power you will be left with none."

Aarja turned her head round and pecked at her back. She pecked out a feather which she gave to Favvo. "Here, have this as a good luck symbol. It's not as potent as the Glittery Stone but it will bring you luck and you will need plenty of that." Then she added, "Be very wary of Nanuk and the Glittery Stone which he wants you to find. He probably has an underlying purpose for you to have it."

Favnir felt overwhelmed. He couldn't believe that this little bird had given him one of her feathers. He managed to stammer out, "Thank you so much, I don't really know what to say." Aarja flew away and left them.

# Chapter Twenty-Two

## Amorok bites Favnir

The spooky sound of wolves howling woke them at dawn. The wolves sounded dangerously close and he worried about Carlo. He knew how scared he was of wolves and understandably, as his mother was killed by one when he was very young. He decided to go out to find Carlo to see if the fox was okay.

He had only walked a short way from the settlement when he heard a whimpering behind a rock. *That fox must have been really scared for him to come so near to the humans.*

Carlo had seen Favnir. "Those wolves are really near. I thought to myself, which is the scarier, humans or wolves? I decided humans were the safer bet as I can outrun them."

Favnir laughed, "You scoundrel. Come back with me and they will see we are friends and they won't harm you. Puja will be especially pleased to see you."

"Okay, I would like to meet Anana and perhaps she could make me a harness so I can ride on your back when we go?"

"You are really determined to come aren't you? But you must have a harness otherwise you can't come. So let's ask her and see what she says."

The two of them walked back to the igloos. It was only a short way and Puja saw them first. She rushed towards them. "Carlo," she cried, "how lovely to see you." She looked as though she wanted to pick him up to give him a hug but Carlo would have none of that and drew back. "Mummy," she called to Anana, "come and meet Carlo."

Anana came out of her igloo with Kiuvuk and Aki behind. By now the sun was up and shining in the sky. The beams of sunlight caught her fair hair and when she looked at Carlo his tail rose up to the sky and he couldn't meet her gaze. He, like Favvo was overcome by her beauty.

Anana spoke, "We've heard so much about you Carlo and it's lovely to actually meet you. I've heard  Flash's stories about how you watched him hatch and then looked after him." She turned back into the igloo and brought out some meat slices for them to eat.

When they had eaten, Carlo gave Favnir a nudge and pointed his head at Anana. Favnir knew what he wanted.

"Carlo really wants to come with me and I have told him the only thing he must have is a harness for him to ride in. Can you make one for him please? Perhaps you could include a small bag as part of it to carry the map. Aarja the bird had given me one of her feathers for luck and it needs to be kept safe as well. Also of course Nanuk has told me to find the Glittery Stone for protection so I will need to keep that safe, so a harness would be really useful"

"Well, that would be a challenge but I think I could do it.  I would have to take measurements and think how to sew it all together. I should be able to finish it in two days. Is that okay?"

"Yes, of course that's fine. Thank you Anana."

Favnir turned to Carlo, "Well, it looks as if we'll be able to go off together on this adventure but I'll understand if you change your mind."

"I won't," Carlo answered. Now that Carlo had met Favnir's human family they decided to go and explore outside. Favnir didn't want to go too far away, he still felt uneasy about meeting Amorok. They aimed for a rocky area that looked interesting and Carlo could play hide and seek with his tail for a while. Carlo couldn't wait to get there and was bouncing ahead when without warning Favnir was attacked by someone who was waiting to ambush him.

It was Amorok. Favnir had no time to defend himself. "Ahrrrr, got you at last. You didn't expect this I bet. My wolves told me where you were and here I am."

Favnir felt a sharp bite on his leg but quickly he threw off the Wolf God and rose on his hind legs in fury. He saw his attacker and blew out his fire. The fire hit Amorok's back and he turned and escaped quickly. Favnir heard him call in triumph.

"I bit you and got some blood. Ha ha, that blood will give me some of your Power and you'll feel so weak." He ran off and left them.

Favnir was in shock. The bite was small and he didn't lose much blood but he felt different, as though he was being drained of energy. The sun and his shadow had gone. Carlo crept out from his hiding place behind a nearby rock.

"That was horrible, Flash. Are you okay?" He saw that Amorok had bitten Favnir and was worried. "Let's go back to the igloos and see if Anana can do anything to help." Favnir managed to crawl very slowly back to the igloos.

Puja saw them and called to her mother. Anana rushed out to meet them and Carlo explained what had happened. Favnir could hardly talk. He collapsed at last outside Anana's igloo and she examined his leg. She went inside and after a while came out with a glass jar filled with a greenish ointment.

"This is a healing balm which was given to me by the same sailor who left the map. It is made from a plant that grows in hot countries over the sea. It has special healing powers. I will try it anyway. It will do no harm." She opened the jar and spread some cream onto Favnir's leg. "Now rest and eat, I will bring you some food and a hot drink."

Soon Favnir fell into a dreamless sleep and in this time Anana measured Carlo for his new harness.

When Favnir woke he felt much better and his leg didn't hurt as much. For the rest of the day and evening he rested and Anana regularly treated his leg with the cream which had a wonderful soothing feel to it. He slept the night through.

# Chapter Twenty-Three

## Anana makes Carlo a saddle

Favnir woke to see Carlo curled up next to him. He smiled to himself and thought, *that fox can be so annoying but I'm glad he's coming with me*. He felt much better, some of his old energy had returned. He lay for a while thinking about his plans. *I will rest today and perhaps Anana will finish Carlo's harness, but I must leave tomorrow, I cannot delay any longer.*

As if Carlo had heard his thoughts, the fox stirred and opened his eyes. He saw Favnir looking at him. "Great, your eyes are seeing me. Yesterday after Amorok's bite you didn't really know where you were and you certainly didn't see me. But I kept with you and told the humans what had happened. I was a real friend."

"Yes, Carlo. You were really helpful and I know you are my friend. Thank you."

Carlo leapt to his feet and his magnificent tail seemed to grow even bigger. "I will dig for some lemmings like in the old days and Anana can cook them this time." He rushed off and eventually returned with three lemmings. They had stopped moving and Carlo rushed over to Anana's igloo and dropped them at the door flap. Carlo could hear movement inside and he called to Anana.

"I've brought breakfast this morning. Look outside." Anana appeared and when she saw the lemmings her face changed. First surprise, followed by dismay, but when she saw Carlo waiting expectantly for her reaction, resignation and finally acceptance.

"Wonderful," she said, "I will skin them and cook them

89

over the fire." She came outside with a knife and board and proceeded to skin the lemmings. Kiuvuk joined her and relit the fire for cooking. Puja and Aki joined them. "Different breakfast this morning children. Carlo has caught some lemmings for us. I'm sure we'll enjoy them."

"This is very good, Carlo," Kiuvuk grunted his approval as he chewed through some meat. Much to Favnir's relief they all agreed that the meat was tasty. Carlo was oblivious. He was very hungry and attacked his breakfast with relish. Favnir did notice though that the humans ate more flat bread than meat.

After breakfast, Anana turned to Carlo and said, "I want to measure you again so you fit into your harness exactly. I don't want you falling off Flash's back for want of a proper support."

Favnir watched through the open door flap as Anana led Carlo into her igloo. At the other end of the igloo was a wooden table with animal skin spread out and a long thin rope with marks at regular intervals. She measured Carlo with this rope, she measured his back together with tail, his shoulder width and his hip width. Eventually she was satisfied and Carlo came outside to join Favnir.

He approved of Anana, "She is very clever and lovely, isn't she?" Favnir didn't want to talk about Anana with Carlo so he grunted and moved away. Although he was feeling better he didn't seem to have much energy and was worried about leaving the next day. "I think I will stay here near the igloo today and rest. My leg is still feeling sore."

As if Anana had heard she appeared with some more soothing balm which she proceeded to massage into Favnir's leg. "I will treat this leg of yours at midday and before you sleep and I'm pretty sure that will do the trick. But I'll give you some of this cream to take with you in case of any emergencies."

Anana went back into the igloo to work on Carlo's harness and Favnir decided he would study the map thoroughly to work out the route he would follow the next day. Carlo thought he would explore again and perhaps have a little adventure.

"Don't go too far Carlo and please be careful. It's not worth taking any risks today."

Anana called to the fox as he scampered off, "Be back mid- afternoon. I will want to see if your harness is the right size."

Favnir spent a relaxing morning studying the map. He thought he had worked out a route and wanted to see if Kiuvuk agreed.

However Favnir was rudely disturbed later in the morning. He saw Carlo on the horizon running frantically towards the igloos. He arrived panting with exertion and looking very frightened. "Guess who I saw, Flash. Wait for it, I was minding my own business and dancing on the snow when I heard this horrible snivelling and I smelt a really awful stench. It was Keelut, that horrible, evil thing of a dog. He was sniffing around and muttering to himself about hunting the dragon. I hid behind a rock and he didn't see me. He moved on in the end and I ran back here. I just wanted to come back, I don't want to come face to face with him again. I had enough last time."

Favnir was horrified, *that means both Amorok and Keelut know I am near here. They just don't know how to give up. They really do want my blood.* Aloud he said, "Okay Carlo, come and sit down near me. Don't worry about Keelut or Amorok, they won't be able to follow me when I'm flying tomorrow. It's Nanuk we have to worry about."

Kiuvuk agreed on Favnir's planned route only suggesting a shorter way at one point. Mid- afternoon Anana fitted the harness onto Carlo and it fitted perfectly. It had a long pocket on one side for the map and two shorter pockets for the feather and cream and the Glittery Stone when they found it.

Favnir gradually began to feel stronger as the day passed. Anana smoothed the healing balm on his wound at midday and before he went to sleep and it seemed to be healing rapidly. He now felt prepared for the next day.

# Chapter Twenty-Four

## Favnir visits Sedna's cairn

Favnir woke early and wondered why he felt so jittery. Then he remembered, he was leaving today to find his father. He stretched and knew his wound was almost healed. He looked at Carlo sleeping next to him and mischievously tweaked his tail. Carlo was immediately awake as Favnir knew he would be. He looked at Favnir indignantly,

"Why did you touch my tail? You know that only I can do that. You are a very naughty dragon." He threw some snow onto Favnir's face.

"Well, little fox, it's time to wake up. Today is our big day and I have to fly roughly 300 miles which is further than I have ever flown. So as soon as the humans are up and we have had something to eat we must go."

Carlo nodded, he knew what was at stake and they both listened for the sounds of movement inside the igloo. They didn't have to wait long because soon Anana appeared at the doorway and washed her hands in the snow with some foamy liquid. Soon after that they could both smell the delicious smell of cooking.

Breakfast was a very sombre meal as Puja was feeling very sad. She didn't want Favnir to leave, she didn't know when she would see him again, if ever. But Favnir and Carlo ate well.

"Well Carlo, it's time for you to be harnessed up." Anana fetched Carlo's harness from inside the igloo. The map fitted exactly into the long side pocket and in the other pocket were Aarja's feather and the healing balm. There was room for the glittery stone in that pocket as well.

Carlo climbed onto Favnir's back. His harness had two clips on either side which fastened onto Favnir's scales perfectly. Carlo was ready. He waved goodbye to the family, not too sad to go.

Anana, Kiuvuk, Aki and Puja all stood near as Favnir prepared to leave. Puja suddenly left her family group and rushed to hug Favnir's leg. "Remember me and come back." She sobbed and returned to Anana's arms.

Favnir looked at Anana and said, "Thanks for everything Anana, I know I will see you again."

Favnir turned and ran several steps flapping his magnificent wings with gathering force. The watching family could feel the great gusts of air which were blown back. They were so powerful that Puja was almost blown to the ground. Eventually he took off and soared into the air. The family watched as the dragon flew higher until he was just a small dot on the horizon and then the dot disappeared.

The sun was shining and Favnir looked for his shadow below. He saw it, clear cut and dark, it was stretching forward and seemed to be leading him. Favnir was content.

Favnir knew by looking at the map that he had to fly South and then East. "Look down Carlo, can you recognise the land here? This is the route you took by yourself in order to find me."

Carlo let out a squeak of excitement. "Yes, over there," and he pointed, "that's where I saw Amorok." Then he added, "He didn't see me, I made sure of that."

Favnir flew steadily on towards the area where he had hatched. Favnir imagined his mother flying over this land and seeing the same things as he was seeing before she had dropped her egg.

Carlo shouted out again. "This is where my mother was killed by those horrible wolves. I don't like this bit, I'll close my eyes until we have left."

Now they were getting near Favvo's hatching place and when Carlo had opened his eyes again he couldn't contain his excitement. "Look over there, I know where we are now. There's the rock I hid behind when I watched you hatch and there is where we saw Nanuk."

It felt very odd to Favnir to fly over this place of his origins. He remembered again his sense of loss and despair when he knew he was alone. He had gained so much since then, his strength, his power of fire, friends in Carlo and Puja and of course he had found his mother. He flew on towards the sea and the region where he had first met the humans. He noticed that it was growing much colder and the snow beneath them was thicker and more widespread. The wind was also gathering force and Favvo found it increasingly hard to fly against it. His shadow had disappeared and Favnir was finding it difficult to feel optimistic.

At last he saw the sea and Favnir knew he had to fly north along the coast.

"Flash, look at the sea. There's so much ice floating about and I can't see much water. It looks so different now."

The water below looked dark and angry and Favnir felt that it did not welcome his presence. The waves were massive and Favnir shuddered when he had a momentary panicky feeling of falling into that water. Favnir heard the wind howling and saw it smashing the waves onto the shore. Out to sea it was smoother and he saw large areas of ice which had joined up and, as Carlo had noticed, covered the water.

Favnir flew slightly inland to find the settlement area. Then they saw it. No humans now and all that was left were the massive whale bones that formed the skeleton of the tents. He decided to take a rest here, he had been flying for a couple of hours and the area was sheltered from the wind. Favnir landed in the centre of the settlement near Puja's old tent.

Carlo unclipped himself and slid off Favnir's back. "Oh, that harness is really safe and comfortable but my bum still needs a rest." He stretched himself and immediately started preening his tail.

They both needed water and food. Anana had managed to pack some meat and flat bread into the space in the harness that would hold the Glittery Stone. They ate half of the food and Favnir used his fire to melt some snow for water. They stopped only for a short time as Favnir wanted to continue his journey. He knew he would have to fly over the cave area where he had searched for his mother. Then of course, he would reach his mother's burial place where he aimed to spend the night.

So when Carlo had climbed onto his back and settled into his harness Favnir flapped his wings and ran into his awe-inspiring leap into the air. Carlo shouted in his excitement. "Wow, I can feel the air trying to push me back. I wouldn't miss this for the world." Again he cried out, "Look Flash, there's the cave where I spent time waiting for you."

He continued his flight and soon they were flying over the cave system. Favnir looked to the sea and saw it was almost totally covered with ice. There were a few patches of water in between the ice floes.

At last they reached Sedna's cave and Favnir saw the stone cairn they had built to cover her body. He called to Carlo. "Hold tight, I'm going to land." He glided down and landed very near where his mother lay.

Favnir had an immediate strange feeling of being welcomed. As he walked closer the feeling got stronger. Carlo left to have a run around and he was left alone with his mother. He placed his two front legs to touch the stones and closed his eyes while he rested. He seemed to disappear into a dark world where he heard Sedna's voice. "*Favnir, we are fused into one body. In that way I will be with you in your quest. Connect with your shadow when you can, that way you will know I am there. You will meet many dangers but never give up. Look at my star at night and in the day feel my strength as well in your shadow. We will win together."*

Her voice faded and Favnir opened his eyes. He saw Carlo returning and the moment was gone.

Carlo had come back with two lemmings and as of old they ate them for supper. But this time Favvo insisted on cooking them with his fire. With them they had two flatbreads which Anana had baked. Favvo had come to like this bread and Carlo suffered it. They slept in the cave entrance near his mother, sheltered by the walls of the cave and lying close together for warmth.

# Chapter Twenty-Five

## Carlo falls down an ice crevice

They both woke at about the same time. They shook themselves to get rid of the fallen snow. Then they walked and jumped about a bit to warm themselves. Favnir opened the pack of food using his teeth and claws. He saw that the food supply was running low. There was only enough for two more meals. *Perhaps this was a time that Carlo could dig for lemmings while I say goodbye to my mother.*

Favnir turned to Carlo and saw that as always the fox was preening his tail. "Carlo, there's not much food left. Go and find some breakfast." Carlo was only too pleased and quickly agreed. He disappeared in search of a likely spot.

Favnir went over to the big pile of stones. He sat down on his back legs and then reached out and felt them. He had no messages from her this time but he did receive comforting vibes.

A few minutes passed and then he heard Carlo shouting out. "Only one this time. But it's a big one which we can share." Favnir stood and still touching the stones said his farewell and left. Carlo had returned first and Favnir heard him panicking.

"Where are you Favnir? I can't see you. Where have you gone?" Then he saw the dragon and gave a sigh of relief. "Don't do that again, I was scared."

"It's okay, Carlo, I was saying goodbye to my mother. I'm ready for breakfast now." He breathed fire onto the lemming and they shared it.

Favnir felt there was something missing and then he

realised what it was. He had felt the lack of wind. It was the first time ever there had been no wind. When he looked at the sky, he saw no clouds and the sky was a dazzling blue. The few scrubby trees cast clear cut shadows on the snow and then he saw his own shadow, dark and menacing. He shook his head in frustration, *no, it's your imagination, this cannot be.*

"Come on Carlo, climb into your harness. I'm ready to fly." Favnir ran some steps and flapped his wings and soon they were airborne. Favnir glanced back at his mother's cairn and he saw that it too cast a striking shadow on the snow but this time he saw splendour and hope.

Favnir continued to fly north. He was aiming for a place called Sydkap. It was from here that he would have to leave land and fly east over the sea to find the island called Vestaris Seamount. It was on this island where he would find his father. It was going to be a long journey north.

All that morning it was easy flying. No wind and the air was clear. They could both see the land beneath in so much detail. For the most part Carlo was silent and absorbed in the landscape. Favvo's wings beat slowly and rhythmically up and down, hypnotic in their regularity. They cast shadows on the snow beneath, moving with the dragon as he flew north.

Now it was definitely getting much colder and clouds were gathering. Favnir saw the land below had more hills and there were fewer bushes and trees. Carlo was growing restless and he called out to Favnir. "Can we stop soon? My bum needs a rest and I am getting hungry."

"Okay, just be patient for a bit longer and we'll stop. We have got to go over those mountains that you can see in the distance. We'll find a spot to rest once we have reached those mountains."

Favnir could feel Carlo wriggling in his harness, shivering with cold but also to make his bum more comfortable. The landscape was becoming more threatening and Favnir could only see snow and ice covering the hills and crevices. Favnir felt a vague foreboding. He could feel that something terrible was about to happen. His shadow appeared to agree as it no longer followed the dragon smoothly, instead it was broken into sharp edges and it seemed to be moving in jerks and then disappearing completely when the sun was covered in the gathering cloud.

They reached the snow covered mountains at last. Favnir heard Carlo give a long sigh of relief. Favvo was looking for a good spot to land. He saw a small valley hemmed in by mountains. He immediately headed that way, wanting desperately to land. To his horror he realised too late that it was hard ice and not snow underfoot. And then to make it worse he saw large cracks in the ice that seemed to disappear into nothing. Favvo just managed to land safely in between two large cracks and he skidded to a halt.

"Okay Carlo, get off my back quickly and stay close. We can't stay long, just time to have a wee and eat something." Carlo was whimpering but managed to release himself from his harness and slid onto the ice. Carlo had retrieved the last of the food from the pouch before he slid off Favnir's back and now he laid it on the ice. They were both hungry and ate it quickly.

Favnir felt the need to stretch his legs. To his horror that movement seemed to start a vibration which Favnir felt as a threat, daring him to stay longer in the ice's territory. That vibration increased to an ear-splitting intensity. Then Favnir heard a sudden deafening clap and Favnir stared, paralysed with shock as the ice crack near Carlo started to widen. Carlo had no time at all to react and jump out of danger. Everything seemed to happen in slow motion. The dragon watched as Carlo was swallowed by the ice into that deep chasm which was getting wider by the second.

Carlo found his voice and Favnir heard him give a shriek of fear and panic as he disappeared. "No..o..o..o." The crack stopped growing wider. Favnir forced himself to move but he found he couldn't think properly. He knew he was panicking and he tried to force himself to think sensibly.

"CARLO", he shouted at the top of his voice. He heard his mother's voice, *calm down, be steady*. Cautiously, Favnir crept on all fours to the spot where Carlo had fallen. Tentatively he peered down; he breathed a sigh of relief. He saw that Carlo had landed on a ledge that he could just about reach. Carlo was curled up in a ball and was shivering with fear. He felt Favnir's breath, so hot it seared through his body and he looked up.

"Oh Flash, you're here. Please save me. I don't want to die down this hole. It's so cold and I'm really frightened." He uncurled himself and when he tried to stand, something caught his eye and he shouted out.

"I can see something glittering. There's a stone stuck in the ice." He started to reach for it and Favnir yelled out, frightened that he might fall off the ledge.

"Be careful Carlo. If you move too quickly you could easily lose your balance and then I could never reach you."

"I'll be careful but I must get this stone. It's so beautiful and sparkly. It could even be the stone that Nanuk wanted you to find."

Favnir watched as Carlo stretched out his neck and took hold of something into his mouth which he dropped onto the ice near him. *How do I rescue Carlo?* He thought of the ropes that Kiuvuk had used at the settlement and wished he had one. *It's not too far down. If I could support myself on this wedge of ice I could lean over and one of my wings could reach him.*

Favnir cautiously leant over the crack and supported himself on the wedge of ice. "Carlo," he called to his friend, "I am leaning down sideways as far I can. I will stretch out my wing to reach you. Climb onto it and cling on as tight as you can. Bring the stone in your mouth."

Carlo was surprisingly calm. He whimpered a bit as he climbed onto Favnir's wing but soon he was on the ice beside Favnir.

He spat out the Glittery Stone onto the ice and they both looked at it with awe as they saw it glitter and sparkle. Carlo hugged Favnir's neck and thanked him over and over. Favnir replied. "You silly fox. I'm glad you're safe and you've found the Glittery Stone. Let's get away from this place now."

Carlo climbed onto Favnir's back, clipped himself into his harness and finally placed the Glittery Stone into its pouch. Favnir flapped his massive wings and soon they were once more in the air.

# Chapter Twenty-Six

## Favnir bonds with his shadow

The sun was shining and Favnir was comforted by the sight of his shadow on the snow beneath where he saw his wings beating rhythmically back and forward, up and down. The wind was behind him now and it was easier flying. Carlo was settled comfortably in his harness and was unusually quiet. Favnir suspected that he had fallen asleep.

Favnir's aim was to fly over the mountains where he hoped for flatter ground. He flew high above the clouds and flew on and on, no longer able to see his shadow. Then he realised that the landscape was altering. The mountains projected a gentler outline against the sky and seemed almost to welcome them. Then they became hills with lovely flat valleys in between. It was still very cold, in fact Favnir realised it was growing colder by the hour. He became aware of movements on his back.

"I didn't think I would fall asleep Flash, I must have been tired. Good job my harness is lovely and secure. It's so comfortable and safe." Then he exclaimed as he looked down, "Oh, we have left the horrible mountains behind. This is much better land. I'm hungry."

Favnir realised he was hungry as well and ready to eat. There was no meat left in their bag, they had only flat bread.

He called to Carlo. "Try and be patient a bit longer. I am looking for a safe place to land. I hope it's a safer place than last time. We have to find food so I am looking for a valley in between the hills." Carlo shouted in reply.

"Perhaps I can dance and find some lemmings. There is

so much snow down there. It feels so cold." Favnir felt him shudder. Soon Favnir saw a secure flat place where he could land. There seemed to be lots of soft snow and he couldn't see much ice. He flew lower, no humans around either. He saw his shadow and reconnected with it by landing.

Carlo released himself quickly and climbed down from Favnir's back onto the snow. The fur on his body and tail was standing up and he looked much bigger.

"That's better," he exclaimed." I don't know why but I feel a lot warmer now with my fur standing up." Favnir looked at him.

"Yes, you are lucky. I can't do that. I will just have to keep moving and make my own heat."

Carlo darted off to have a wee and sniff the snow for lemming smells. He soon called to Favnir who was moving about to keep warm. "Found a smell. OK lemmings, here I come." He did his amazing dance and found two lemmings."

Favnir produced some fire and soon they were eating cooked lemming.

"You know what Carlo? I think we both need to stay here awhile. I reckon I have flown 300 miles today and it's a safe spot. We'll stay here overnight. I want to look at the map and look at that stone again, I want to know what it does."

Carlo climbed onto Favnir's back and reached into the harness. He found the map and using his mouth threw it onto the snow. Favnir peered at it and after a while managed to find roughly where they were.

"Look Carlo, I think we are about here and he pointed with his claw. I think we have to fly a good 350 miles tomorrow to reach Sydkap. Let's hope there is a light wind.

There might be some more mountains to fly over as well. That is a human settlement so we must be careful. We can rest there before we make the sea journey to find the island of Vestaris Seamount. Now can you put the map back and throw the stone down so we can look at it again?"

Carlo threw the stone onto the ground and they poured over it, prodding and feeling it. Favnir felt a strong feeling that he couldn't explain sweep over him as he stroked it. A sensation of being swept away into nothingness and at the same time absorbing power. Perhaps he was imagining it. He saw something he hadn't noticed before.

Look Carlo, do you see those tiny holes at this end? I wonder why they are there. Perhaps we'll find out later. Put it back now and then let's sleep. We can start at dawn, we have a long journey tomorrow."

# Chapter Twenty-Seven

## Carlo makes friends with Cora

When they started flying the next day Favnir immediately realised there was no wind, which was good. Then he saw low clouds and he realised he couldn't see his shadow. That made him feel insecure. But he flew on and two hours passed. Carlo started twitching in his harness.

"Can we stop soon Flash? I need a stretch and a wee."

"Very soon. I would like to fly a bit further. I can tell by the angle of the sun that we are not yet halfway. We have to keep going for now."

Carlo accepted that with a grunt and settled down again. Favnir flew on and on. When Favnir judged they were about halfway to Sydkap he started looking for a place to land. Now they were in a long flat valley between high hills. There were trees on the lower slopes of the hills. Favnir saw a small herd of Caribou grazing on tufts of grass that were exposed above the snow. Eventually he saw a spot near some low rocks and away from the Caribou. Relieved he saw his shadow, the outline was a bit blurred but he reconnected with it and landed.

"We mustn't stay too long Carlo. There is still just over 100 miles to fly and soon it will be dusk."

"Okay, I get that. I will see if there is anything else that I can catch to eat." Carlo disappeared behind the rocks and away from the dragon. Favnir expected him to be back soon but he didn't return. He gave the fox more time but he was getting worried and itching to go. He climbed one of the rocks and called.

"Where are you Carlo? If you don't come back soon, I

will have to try to find you."

Favnir gave him a little more time and then decided to fly over the area. He found him not far away. But he was not alone. He had found a friend. The fox was as white as Carlo but had brown patches on her shoulders. They were playing together in the snow, chasing each other round and round. He was really enjoying himself. Then he saw Favnir and stopped chasing.

"Oh sorry Flash. I was looking for food. But I have found a friend instead. Meet Cora, isn't she lovely?" Cora cowered down low, terrified of this fearsome creature.

Hello Cora, I'm not as terrible as I look and Carlo is my friend and we are on a mission. Would you mind if he came with me and we would promise to come back again when we return?"

Cora nodded nervously but Carlo had another idea. "We still have to find food. Perhaps Cora and I could find something together and then find you here. Will you wait a few minutes Flash?" Favnir had to agree and the two foxes went off together.

They did return as promised with a dead arctic hare. Cora was astonished to see Favnir produce fire for cooking but joined in to eat it. Then almost reluctantly Carlo left Cora and climbed into the harness to fly away, a bit late but better than never.

By the time they saw the settlement of Sydkap it was dark. Below him Favnir saw wooden huts and streets and a few humans walking around on their two feet. They didn't look up to see the dragon above with his fox passenger. The moon was a new one and cast little light. Favnir flew over the settlement and very soon saw an empty space to land.

Carlo slept under Favnir's wing and dreamt of Cora.

# Chapter Twenty-Eight

## Favnir nears his father's island

The eerie red glow of the rising sun woke them. Favnir looked back and saw the settlement in the distance with a few humans appearing at the doors of their shelters. He could smell the sea and he knew it was near.

"We must start soon Carlo, before the humans wake completely. Let's grab some of that flatbread and go. I'm so glad that Anana gave us lots of that. We can perhaps rest on an island and find something else on the way." Favnir wouldn't even let Carlo preen his tail.

Carlo climbed onto the dragon's back and found his harness. His questing paw felt the glittery stone and it made him feel very odd, dizzy almost. He quickly withdrew his paw and threw a slice of bread to Favnir.

"I don't know what that stone is Flash, but it had a strange effect when I stroked it. It made me feel weird."

Favnir made no comment but he thought, *I must find out more about this stone. Before I use it I must know what it does.* He turned his thoughts inward to ask his mother but had no reply.

"OK, let's go." Yet again he made his pre- run to take off, flapping his wings as he ran. They were soon in the air making for the sea. Favnir knew it would be a long flight of just over 200 miles and he desperately hoped that there was some small islands where they could land to rest.

There were enormous ice floes on the dark grey sea, sometimes so large they looked like land. There were massive waves which crashed onto the surrounding ice. After they had flown for nearly an hour Carlo shifted in his harness and shrieked out in excitement.

"Look Flash, look down. There are sea animals climbing onto that small ice block."

"Yes, I can see that and look, there are other larger sea creatures trying to catch them. You can see they are black and white and very strong. I want to see what's happening. I'm going to circle round a bit." Favnir lowered one wing and reversed his flight path, he flew lower and saw the animals in the water grouping themselves together and crashing into the ice floe. They did this several times until the ice started to break and the small creatures fell in the water. They were then an easy meal for the large creatures.

As Carlo watched he grew more and more agitated. "I don't like this at all. If I fell into that water those black and white animals could easily catch me."

"I think those small animals are the sort that Kiuvuk caught, they are seals. I don't know what the others are, but I think they might be a type of whale. Aki talked about them once."

Favnir reversed back to his original path and flew on. Another hour passed and Favnir was beginning to despair of finding anywhere to rest. Then he saw a protrusion of land on the horizon. "We'll make for that," He shouted to Carlo. When he reached it Favnir looked down and saw no humans, only scrubby bushes showing their green shoots through the snow. It was a small island but it would do. He landed near the sea and as he flew down he saw activity near the surface. *Fish*, he thought, they *will do nicely for a meal.*

Carlo practically fell out of his harness and onto the ground. He rushed into the scrub for a wee, Favnir didn't have the need; he could hold his wee for much longer. Favnir went to look at the sea, he peered between the ice floes and saw some fish. He was an expert at fishing now and soon he had caught four fish which he cooked using his fire. The dragon and the little fox sat down on the ice and ate roasted fish. They wanted to rest for longer but Favnir wanted to find his island in the light and the days were now very short.

"Okay Carlo, we have about two hours before it gets dark. I hope we can find another island on the way. Vestaris Seamount has a special shape so we should be able to recognise it. Kiuvuk told me that it used to be a volcano under the sea and it rose above the water to become an island. It has a flat top to it and very steep sides. It's in the Greenland Sea halfway between Greenland and a big island called Iceland. There are no humans on the Mount but hopefully my father will be there. Let's go."

More flying and another hour passed. Then Carlo saw another island. Once again they flew low and Favnir chose a good place to land near the shore. As he descended he saw his shadow lengthening and more blurred but he managed to reconnect and landed for a brief rest.

Very soon they were in the air again and this time Favnir was looking for an island with a flat-topped mountain. They were both impatient now to find it. Both of them were suffering from tiredness and the intense cold. It was also rapidly getting dark.

"I so wish we had taken one of those skin coverings that the humans used. That would be lovely to curl up in one of those." Carlo mumbled to himself. Then he noticed something.

"What's that over there? To the right and just on the horizon. It must be an island and it looks as if there is a huge mountain with a flat top." As always Carlo with his clear vision had seen the island before Favnir.

Favnir looked to the right and saw a blurred mound in the distance. He changed direction and excitedly increased the speed of his wing beat. As he got closer he was sure that this was the island called Vestaris Seamount. Almost all of the island was a huge mountain and it had a flat top. Thankfully they had found it while it was still light. It would be totally dark in another half hour.

Circling round and looking down to find a safe place to land, Favnir realised that the approaching darkness had taken away his shadow. That troubled him but Favnir heard his mother's voice reassuring him. *"Don't worry, your shadow will appear tomorrow. It always goes away overnight."*

Favnir saw a rocky cove with a flat beach and he swooped down to land. As he did so he felt a huge bubble of happiness. He gave a little skip of excitement and a dragon whoop of joy. He had arrived on his father's island, he had almost achieved his aim which was to find his father.

# Chapter Twenty-Nine

## Testing time for Favnir

After the immediate elation, exhaustion took over and both Favnir and Carlo dropped to the ground and slept. It was early dawn when they were both woken by a loud, discordant rumbling noise. Favnir leapt to his feet and thought at first that the ground was cracking open again to swallow them up.

Carlo was awake as well. "What's that noise Flash? It sounds like thunder but there's no lightning." Favnir knew that the sound was not thunder, but he was puzzled. The rumbling continued and he found he wanted to join in. Then he realised what it was.

"That's not thunder Carlo, that's the sound of dragons waking up. I know now where they are on the mountain. We'll go there as soon as we have eaten. Let's go down to the sea to fish."

Carlo's tail was drooping and his ears flat. "I think we need some luck, those dragons didn't sound too friendly and look out there, the sea is covered with ice."

"Perhaps it's time we used Aarja's feather then. Can you fetch it from the harness?" Carlo leapt up to get the feather and returned with it in between his teeth. "Now put it under the biggest scale on my right shoulder. That should bring us luck. Let's go down to the sea."

Carlo was right, the sea was totally covered in ice. *What do we do now?*

Carlo shouted out. "Look over there, that's amazing." Favnir looked in the direction in which Carlo had pointed and he watched a seal came up through the ice AND he had some fish in his mouth. Carlo felt a cunning plan unfolding in his head. He nudged Favnir to get behind a large rock so the seal didn't see the dragon. He then scampered over to the seal and called to him.

"Hiya, nice to meet you. You look as if you were really lucky to catch those fish. I bet you don't do that every day" As Carlo expected, the seal took immediate offence.

"It isn't luck at all. I use a special technique. I find a soft spot in the ice and when I catch the fish I come up on the ice and eat them. Easy!"

"Prove it then, I bet you couldn't do it again." The seal was really conceited but not terribly intelligent. He forgot about caution and just wanted to show off.

"Course I could, I'll show you." He dived off the ice into the water and disappeared, leaving his first catch of fish on the ice. It was just what Carlo had planned. As soon as the seal had gone Carlo leapt onto the fish and soon they were in his mouth.

Favnir couldn't believe what he had seen. He came out from hiding to meet Carlo. "That seal is going to be angry. We had better take these fish back from the shore a bit." When they were near the rocks Carlo spat the fish onto the ice. Favnir used his fire to cook them, they were delicious.

"Right, let's go and find these dragons. From now on I will keep Aarja's feather under my scale, it certainly seems to bring us luck." They were still hearing the dragon's thunder; it was coming from the centre of the island near the top of the steep slope of the Mount. Full daylight was approaching and Favnir was filled with renewed confidence.

As they flew nearer to the centre of the Mount the thundery noises were almost deafening. Carlo whimpered and cowered back in his harness. Favnir noticed the surrounding rocks were sharp and angular and almost black in colour. Eventually they were almost stopped by a sheer cliff and the only way through was a narrow crevice which looked just wide enough for Favnir to fly through.

"I'm going through Carlo, hang on tight. When we reach the other side make yourself scarce. I've a feeling you had better hide. I will meet the dragons alone."

Carlo was all too ready to agree. At last they emerged on the other side and saw a system of caves ahead. Favnir landed and Carlo slipped off his back whispering to Favnir, "I will unclip the harness and hide it under this rock. Don't forget the Glittery Stone is there." Favnir nodded and Carlo disappeared out of sight, deciding to hide among the rocks for a while.

Favnir looked for his shadow but found it difficult to find. There were so many high rocks obscuring the sun. He approached the caves and suddenly an enormous dragon appeared. He was dark grey in colour and he postured menacingly in front of Favnir.

"A strange dragon appearing without warning! Declare yourself stranger, our den is not to be approached lightly." He flapped his gigantic wings as he spoke and made himself look even bigger.

Favnir replied. "Who are you? You are very rude to a stranger who has travelled many miles to find his father."

The dragon leapt up onto a nearby rock. He now looked down on Favnir making his appearance even more threatening. "How dare you reply to me like that? I am Kiddra, the brother of our leader. You are an upstart youngster. You will have to be put in your place. What do you mean by finding your father?"

Favnir was determined not to be undermined. "My name is Favnir and my mother is Sedna. Look at my stripes. Do they not remind you of her?"

Kiddra peered at him and Favnir saw him give a start of recognition. "I suppose you have a right to find your father," he said grudgingly. "He is ill and not able to meet you here. You will have to enter the caves but before you have the honour of meeting him you will have to pass the qualifying tests. These tests were thought necessary many years ago to prevent strange dragons entering our nest.

The first test is in the form of a riddle, then there are three more tests within the caves."

"I'm ready." Favnir walked closer to his uncle.

"This is the riddle, your first task." He glared at Favnir, challenging him to solve it.

I am sometimes wide and sometimes thin,
You may not leave if you dare go in
My world is darkness, fear and dread
Where the sun can't shine
Until the Dragon's dead.
What am I?

When Favnir heard this he was confused. He kept telling himself he had to solve the riddle before he would be allowed to enter the cave. He knew this but he was panicking and couldn't think straight. Then he heard Sedna's voice. *Calm down and think hard. It's got to be somewhere you can enter and then it's dark and the sun can't shine.* But then he thought, *I can't leave unless the dragon is dead. Which dragon, is it me? Kiddra obviously doesn't want me to go into the cave, he's trying to put me off.* Then with a flash of understanding he shouted out.

"I know the answer. It's this Dragon's Cave."

Kiddra grunted and shifted on his feet. Favnir thought he looked extremely unhappy and he knew he had given the right answer. Kiddra gave another grunt. "Unfortunately I must let you go into the cave, but be prepared for three more tough tests before you are allowed to meet your father."

Favnir proceeded into the cave and was met with a dark cavernous space. It was dimly lit by several greasy sticks emitting a faint but defiant light. So far so good but he was expecting Test one at any time. He walked on to the far end where the cavern narrowed to form a tunnel. The tunnel was dimly lit by the same fatty sticks. The floor of the tunnel was sheer ice but it had a pattern incised into it. This pattern was made of squares. As Favnir watched he saw that the squares were continuously moving. They took turns to open up into black space and Favnir realised that if he trod on one that was going to change, he would fall into an inescapable pit. *Okay, carefully does it*. It was difficult to keep his balance on the smooth ice. *Think of your mum and of Aarja's feather*. He almost fell but just saved himself. As he regained his balance he noticed that just before a square opened it flashed at one corner. All he had to do was to look for the flashes. He painstakingly progressed through the configuration and at last he reached the end of the tunnel. Favnir had passed the first test.

Beyond the tunnel was a large round cave. This cave was even colder and the cold constricted Favnir's muscles so that it was hard for him to walk. He had to pant to work up heat in his mouth but he found he could not produce his fire. There were groups of white needle like shapes hanging from the ceiling. They were made of ice and they reached to the floor. They were pointed at the ends He tentatively felt one end and nearly cried out in pain. The sharp point had actually penetrated his scale. The needles surrounded Favnir on all sides and he could see no way out of the cave.

Whenever he approached a group to see if there was a way out they moved and criss crossed themselves to form an impenetrable curtain. If Favnir went too close he felt their edges cutting again at his scales. *Keep calm.* He heard Sedna's voice in his head. Favnir walked very slowly around the cave looking at each group of needles carefully. After he had walked twice round the cave he realised that the groups varied in size. One group was definitely smaller than the others and had smaller and less sharp ends. Favnir slowly approached this group and peered through the needles. He saw a dim shape which he thought looked like a rock outcrop. Then he saw a gap just large enough for him to squeeze through. These needles did not close to prevent him, instead they opened to make it easier.

*Mum, I have made it. I have passed the second test. There is only one more test to do.* He left the cave of needles and made for the rock outcrop.

As he approached, Favnir saw that there were in fact two rocks facing each other and guarding a passage leading to another cave. Suddenly Favnir thought of Carlo hiding outside these caves and although he missed his company and continual optimism, he was glad he wasn't here. He wouldn't have coped with this extreme cold and these awful challenges.

Favnir walked slowly and carefully into the next cave and immediately came to a halt. He stared around not able to fully believe what he saw. The walls were sheer ice and the ice acted as mirrors. For the first time ever he saw his own image. And it wasn't just one image, everywhere he looked he saw a reflection of himself. He knew it was him because every action he did was mirrored in the images. He put a foreleg out to touch the ice and it was as if he had touched himself. He flexed one wing and the image did the same. *Now Favnir, which ice panel is hiding the exit?* He walked around examining all the ice mirrors. They all looked the same. Favnir began to panic. *Look for your shadow Favnir.* He heard his mother's voice and he was encouraged to study the floor, desperately searching for his shadow. It was very dim but suddenly a sunbeam filtered through the roof of the cave through a crack in the surrounding rock. That particular cave must be positioned near the surface. At last he found his rather blurred shadow, it pointed to one ice panel and so Favnir moved to face that panel. He saw a small catch on one side which he pushed and it opened to reveal yet another tunnel. Wow, Favnir had passed all three tests.

Favnir felt that he had now earned his true name and was ready to meet his father.

Holding his breath he walked along the short passage until it opened up to reveal an enormous hall. He saw a rocky bench at the far end with an old dragon using it for rest. The cave was lit by the same greasy sticks. There were four more dragons in the cave surrounding the one on the bench. It seemed to Favnir that they were protecting him.

He heard Sedna's voice. *Oh Hogruth, my mate and my leader, you have grown so old since I last saw you. I too am old. I am only a star in the sky now but I am still a part of your son, Favnir.* The old dragon had also heard Sedna's voice and was now peering at Favnir through short sighted eyes, trying to see him clearly.

Favnir could not believe that he had at last found his father. Could this dragon really be Hogruth? He stood stock still unable to move, staring at this dragon. He still needed proof. Was this dragon going to accept him as his son?

# Chapter Thirty

## Favnir meets his father

Hogruth's eyes lit up with new interest.

"And who are you, who dares to enter this cave of dragons? Whoever you are, you must have solved the riddle and overcome the dangers of the entrances."

In response Favnir came closer and turned himself sideways so that Hogruth could see his stripes. He heard his father give a gasp. "You have the same colours as Sedna. You must be my son and Sedna is your mother. I thought I was imagining that voice in my head but this is proof. How can this be?"

"Yes Father, Sedna is my mother. I am Favnir. She dropped my egg in the wastes of Greenland when she was ill. I managed to find her in the end." Hogruth interrupted him.

"How is she? Is she well? I sent her on a dangerous mission and I really regret that now."

Favnir had to tell him that Sedna had died and he and his human friends had buried her on the shores of East Greenland. Hogruth's head drooped and his tail dropped even more when he heard this news. But then he realised what Favnir had just said.

"Human friends, how can that be? That's wonderful if it's true. At last we have made friendly contact with the humans. My son, how have you achieved this?"

Favnir told him the whole story. As he spoke Hogruth laid down on his bench and closed his eyes. Favnir thought he had dropped off to sleep but when he had finished his story he opened his eyes and looked at Favnir intently.

"You have done all this, I am proud of you Favnir. Stories have been passed down that a dragon would be hatched one day who would lead us back to the humans. I think you could be the one."

Favnir was aware of movement at the back of the cave. He looked round and saw Kiddra glaring at him. Favnir thought, *I might have been accepted by my father but my uncle is not convinced. He is still wary of me and hates me because I am different.*

Hogruth spoke. "Come, you must be hungry." He asked one of the younger dragons to bring out some meat. It was seal meat and Favnir suddenly realised that he was famished. He wolfed it down and Hogruth then spoke.

"I will tell you the Dragon story and why we are here.

Many years ago, dragons used to live freely with humans. These humans accepted us in those days and we guided them towards peace with each other. There were about fifty of us around the world living on mountain tops. The humans can be rather silly and they would argue with each other for no real reason. If left to themselves they would actually go to war and kill each other. For many years we lived side by side with respect. But one day a dragon was born who wanted more power. He got angry sometimes with the humans and started to kill them if they didn't obey him. The humans started to fear and avoid us. We couldn't guide them anymore and wars broke out all over the planet. That dragon had more offspring who were also fierce and warlike. Peace loving dragons separated off to live apart and kept to themselves. But sometimes even in those groups an evil dragon would be born.

Now there are only about thirty dragons left. We are a group of nine, it was ten with Sedna. My brother Kiddra, you have met; there he is at the back of the cave. He can be somewhat overpowering but he takes my place sometimes. Here is my other son and his two females. There are four more females two of whom live outside, they seem to prefer to be in the air however cold it is."

When he had heard all this Favnir was silent for a long time. This story was hard to hear, he wanted time to think about it. He still wanted to know why his mother had left and what mission she was on when she dropped her egg above Greenland. Hogruth hadn't explained that. He glanced back and saw that Kiddra had left the cave. Favnir wondered where he had gone.

Favnir spoke. "That's quite a story Father. My mother said you would explain everything. I know she is still with me, I sometimes hear her speaking to me inside my head. But now tell me why Sedna was sent on this mission. What was her task?"

Hogruth opened his mouth and was just about to speak when there was a commotion at the back of the cave. Favnir heard Kiddra roaring with rage and then he heard Carlo whimpering with fear. He looked round and there was the image he never hoped to see. Kiddra was dragging Carlo into the cave by his tail.

"See what I have here," roared Kiddra. He threw Carlo down in front of Hogruth. "Here is an animal that Favnir must have brought with him. He was skulking around outside foraging under a rock when I saw him and now he has something in his mouth that he will not give me. Horrible creature, he almost tripped me up. He must be executed at once."

Favnir stepped forward. "I brought him with me and he is my friend. He is an Arctic Fox and his name is Carlo. Release him at once and Carlo, bring me the object you have in your mouth." Favnir had seen the glitter in Carlo's mouth and knew what it was.

Hogruth repeated Favnir's order. Kiddra reluctantly released Carlo. He skidded on the ground and came to a stop near Favnir. Favnir knew the fox had been hurt. Carlo spat the stone out and Favnir quickly gathered it up into his mouth and placed it behind one of his wing scales. Carlo was trembling both with fear and indignation that his tail had been molested by Kiddra.

"Don't worry Carlo, I will protect you." Favnir tried to reassure the little fox.

Kiddra was roaring with fury and indignation. "That miserable fox has no business here. He should never have come. Favnir should never have brought him to our den. I demand that he be killed. He will bring us all bad luck."

Favnir noticed that Hogruth was quiet and didn't say anything to support his son. *He is dominated by my uncle. My father is weak and Kiddra is waiting for him to die and then he will take over the rule of the dragons' nest.*

Favnir intervened. "Carlo will not be killed. He is harmless and has been a true friend to me. When I first hatched he cared for me and taught me how to survive. I will not stand by and see him executed for no real reason."

Kiddra stamped heavily over to Favnir and glowered down into Favnir's eyes. Favnir stood his ground and stared back.

"You young upstart, how dare you challenge me. Now I'm challenging you to a combat over this. It will be a fight to the death. Tomorrow at dawn we will fight outside the cave. That fox's life is the prize."

Favnir lowered his eyes and looked at Carlo trembling at his feet. *I never thought it would come to this. Me fighting my uncle. He is stronger and bigger than me. Could I possibly win?*

He heard his mother's voice. *Know that I am with you in this. I know Hogruth's brother, he will use many dirty tricks to win and he is strong. Remember the Glittery Stone.*

Favnir made his decision. He raised his eyes to meet those of his uncle's. "That's fine by me. I will fight you at dawn tomorrow."

# Chapter Thirty-One

## Favnir fights his uncle and meets Elke

One of the female dragons took Carlo away. Favnir saw that she was gentle with him but Favnir heard the fox whimpering as he was led away and he cast imploring looks in Favnir's direction.

Favnir hardly slept at all that night. He was trying to think of a plan to outwit Kiddra. He knew he could not win by strength alone. He kept rubbing the Glittery Stone and he felt stronger by just touching it. He found the small holes that he had noticed before. Again he asked himself, *I wonder what these are for.* He also took out Aarja's feather and sniffed it. He hoped it would bring him luck the next day.

The sun at last appeared on the horizon. The other dragons stirred and woke. Favnir couldn't face food, he only drank water.

Favnir was led outside by a young dragon. It was not through the tortuous entrance but a shorter exit which led through a simple passage to the outside. He was greeted by an awe inspiring sunrise. Red, orange, pinks and indigo all combined together to blast his senses. The colours dominated the sky and it seemed that the colours were giving Favnir a message of strength.

He saw Carlo being led out by a young female dragon. The fox was told to sit a short distance away so he could see the fight. Favnir could see he was trembling with a combination of fear and worry. He knew his very life depended on Favnir winning the combat. Favnir still had the Glittery Stone under his scale. He managed to get hold of it and he threw it to Carlo.

"Keep it safe Carlo, I might need it."

Favnir crouched low on the ground and waited. He was motionless; as still as the very rocks which surrounded them. As he waited he had a glimpse of two female dragons he hadn't seen before. They were waiting in the background and one in particular caught his eye. She kept looking from side to side and stroking her flank as if she was worried.

Then he heard deafening roars from the approaching dragon. When Kiddra emerged from the tunnel his appearance was as he had intended, formidable and terrifying. He was bigger and stronger than Favnir and he seemed to tower over him. His neck and shoulders were enclosed in strong armour. He started flapping his great wings to create a strong wind around Favnir to try to disorientate him. Roaring with menace he made a sudden dive for Favnir's neck who was still waiting motionless. But Favnir was expecting this attack and he turned sharply to one side. Favnir waited again; he waited and waited, still not moving. Kiddra circled round Favnir continually bellowing with rage. Favnir watched, always keeping a close eye on Kiddra and trying to foretell his next move.

Kiddra suddenly tried to pounce onto Favnir from behind but again Favnir anticipated this move and unexpectedly stood up to his full height and twisted round to face Kiddra. Now Favnir bellowed out his challenge. The air vibrated with the sound of the two dragons venting their wrath until the air was full and could take no more. Carlo covered his ears. Again and again Kiddra tried to jump onto Favnir's back and again and again Favnir thwarted him. Favnir lowered himself onto the ground and crawled underneath Kiddra's belly. He wanted to bite his soft under part. Kiddra tried to breathe fire onto Favnir but couldn't manage the right position and he roared with frustration. In the end he somehow managed to breathe fire onto Favnir's left wing. Favnir was badly wounded and in pain but he managed to breathe his fire onto Kiddra's belly and now there were two wounded dragons but Kiddra was still the bigger and stronger.

They were both roaring with anger, breathing fire in all directions. The smell of fire pervaded the compound. But the sun was at its full strength and Favnir at last saw his shadow. He knew Carlo's life was at stake and he heard Sedna's voice. *Kiddra has a weak spot in his neck. That is why his neck is covered with armour. Throw the Glittery Stone at his neck.* Favnir shouted at Carlo to tell him to shove the stone over to him. Favnir then kicked it into Kiddra's neck and he watched the results with amazement. The stone seemed to melt the armour and Kiddra's neck was open to attack.

With one enormous leap Favnir landed on Kiddra's back and he bit hard into his neck. Kiddra refused to give up and he twisted violently trying to throw Favnir off his back. But Favnir clung on and bit again and again into the same vulnerable spot until Kiddra collapsed onto the icy ground. Favnir loomed over him and there was still hate in Kiddra's eyes as he gazed up at him, now dying on the snow.

Favnir spoke to Kiddra, "You gave me no choice. You are my uncle and I didn't want to kill you but I had to protect Carlo. He is my friend and always will be." He collected the stone from Kiddra's neck and kicked it to Carlo.

As Kiddra lay dying Favnir went over to Carlo. "You are free but I think it would be best if you respected the dragons and kept away from the cave. Keep near and I will contact you soon. Keep the stone safe."

Carlo gave Favnir one grateful and awestruck look and scampered away into the rocks.

Favnir approached Hogruth. "I've won this battle and now you are free from your controlling brother. You can rule as you wish. I think we have to talk about the future."

Hogruth stumbled as he stood and his face was twitching with emotion. Favnir could see that his father was very weak. This time he took the lead and guided his father back into the cave where he collapsed onto the ledge which served as his throne. Favnir, although exhausted himself and in terrible pain, tried to care for his father. One dragon appeared laden with meat and fruits. She also brought a bowl of a deep red liquid.

"Drink some of this," she indicated the liquid and passed the bowl to Hogruth first. "It will give you both back your strength."

Hogruth drank deeply and gratefully and he perked up immediately. He sat up straight and looked Favnir in the eyes. Favnir sipped cautiously at first and then drank all that was left of the liquid. He felt a burning sensation travel through his body and up to his wings and head. Whatever was in that liquid was sensational. He felt almost like another fight! He returned Hogruth's stare and spoke.

"Now just tell me everything else I need to know. Why was my mother flying over Greenland and where she was going?"

This time Hogruth spoke without interruption. "Your mother Sedna was a beautiful dragon and she was my favourite of all the females. Kiddra was a worry. He was growing more demanding in his ways and questioning my authority. I felt that he was dominating me. There are two more dragon settlements on the planet. Sedna offered to fly to the other dragon settlements to find out how many tyrants there are left. When she started her journey she didn't know that she carried an egg. I would like to see us make peace with the humans and live as we used to. She was not feeling very strong when she left, perhaps she had an accident on the way and that made her much weaker. But I have heard that there are two big settlements left and they are ruled by angry dictators who call themselves The Cohort of Dragons".

Favnir nodded. He had noticed a small gash on his mother's side when they were burying her. She could have caught herself on a rock when she was landing at some point in time.

"I will take my mother's place and fly to these places. I want to do this, I feel it's my destiny. If necessary I will fight these evil dragons as I fought Kiddra. I will rid the world of these evil creatures. Then we will have the good dragons back and we can live openly with humans again."

Hogruth grunted with approval, he had hoped that Favnir would react like this.

"I will stay here for a few more days to make sure I am fully grown. Carlo will not come into the cave but I must find him and I know he will want to come with me. But there is one more thing I want to do. Tomorrow I will go outside to find a certain female who I saw watching me fight. I must get to know her."

Hogruth grunted again with even more approval and Favnir understood that he had his father's support.

The next day Favnir walked out of the cave with two purposes in his mind. The first was to find Carlo and the second to find the female dragon who he knew was living outside the cave. He stood still for a few minutes, undecided who to find first. The decision was made for him because as he stood there he caught a glimpse of movement behind a large boulder, he was being watched. Favnir walked over to the boulder. He stood casually and looked around as if he didn't know where to go. Then a beautiful female dragon appeared before him.

"Hi, I watched you fight that awful Kiddra yesterday. I was with you all the way. He's the reason my friend and I live in the open. We couldn't bear to be near him, he was really nasty. My name is Elke, what's yours?"

Favnir wanted to impress this lovely female. He rose to his full height and breathed some fire before he replied. "I am Favnir, Protector of the Weak. I have a friend who you may have seen yesterday who calls me Flash. He is a tiny Arctic Fox who has proved to be my true friend. Are you related to Hogruth?"

"No, I was living with a small group of dragons in a country called Italy. But the leader who is called Draakon, is even more vicious than Kiddra. Much as I liked the hot temperatures there I decided to find this group. I had heard about this settlement from general gossip. My friend, Anneka flew for the same reason from even further afield from a place called Mexico."

Favnir decided he liked Elke very much. He liked her even more when she said,

"If you are looking for your friend, I know where he is. He's not far and the last time I saw him he was grooming his tail. He's very vain, isn't he? Follow me, I'll take you."

Elke was right. Favnir soon spotted Carlo. His black nose stood out against the snow and he was still grooming his tail. Elka stood back as the two greeted each other. Carlo was overjoyed to see Favnir and was soon prancing around and swishing his tail backwards and forwards. Favnir spread his wings out to show Carlo how much they had grown in the little time he had been here.

"Flash, you are massive and your wings are huge. You were wonderful yesterday, I was so proud of you. But who is this?"

"This is Elke. Isn't she lovely? She's already my special friend."

Carlo's ears drooped and his tail dropped and trailed in the snow. Favnir noticed, "Don't worry Carlo, nobody will replace you but you have a special friend waiting for you and now I have too." Carlo cheered up when he heard this.

"Have you still got the Glittery Stone and keeping it safe? I have the feather tucked behind my neck scale."

"Yes, I have. I have a feeling we will need these when we go travelling again in a few days."

Favnir told Carlo all that Hogruth had told him and that he would fly round the world to find the other dragon groups and challenge any evil dragons.

"Another adventure then. I can't wait."

# Chapter Thirty-Two

## Favnir's new plan

Favnir looked at the little fox sadly. *He has no idea how dangerous this 'adventure' will be. I could easily get killed and he would be marooned all by himself. We are going to hotter countries and he will not like the weather.*

He spoke to Carlo. "I don't know how to say this Carlo, I'm really worried about taking you this time. Something could easily happen to me. What would you do? I am going to warmer countries and you won't like that. No digging for lemmings."

Carlo jumped back when he heard this and his tail drooped. "Do you really mean this Flash? I can't believe you are saying it. I must go with you."

"We have a couple of days before I fly to another strange land. Anana's map won't help this time. I think my father will be able to suggest some directions. We have to think about this very carefully. You see, I could take you back to Greenland and drop you off to meet up with Cora."

Carlo's eyes lit up with interest when he heard this. "That would be good," he admitted. "But," he added, "I would still want to come with you."

Favnir thought all that evening and most of the following day about what to do. Hogruth was helpful and he decided he would go to Italy first and find the smoking mountain which was in the south. After that he would probably come back to the Mount to rest before he went to Mexico.

He had thought of a brilliant plan. When he had finished talking to his father about the journey, he came out of the cave and found Carlo.

"How about this Carlo. We'll travel together to Italy and return to the Mount to rest. After that we'll travel to Greenland and I'll see you are reunited with Cora. Then I will go to Mexico by myself. As I said before it will be very dangerous and if anything happens to me, you will be by yourself." He hardly dared breathe as he waited for Carlo's response.

"That sounds like a good plan. I'll go along with that." Favnir breathed a silent sigh of relief.

"Right, we have one more day to prepare." Favnir had to go over directions again with his father. He had to make sure he took food with him for four days travel and ensure that the harness was still secure for Carlo. As he had no need for Anana's map he would leave it with Hogruth. But he would definitely take the healing cream, the Glittery Stone and the feather.

The afternoon's bright sunlight drew him outside. He saw his shadow, clear-cut and comforting. He looked down at himself. *Yes, I have reached full size and power now*. He spread his wings and saw how magnificent they were; he flapped them and caused an enormous gust of wind to sweep across the mouth of the cave. He heard his mother's voice. *You are such a magnificent creature my son. I am so proud of you. You are capable of wonderful things. I will always travel with you.*

Favnir looked round and saw Elke. Her head was drooping and her colour was fading as he gazed at her. Favnir walked over and stood close. "I will be back and we will get to know each other very well." He held his head high and said with conviction, "Don't worry about me, I will return." She nodded calmly and walked away.

Favnir watched her go and thought. *I think I could*

*really love this dragon. She is so calm and comforting. Elke never seems to panic and she would be good for me in difficult situations. She doesn't talk much but what she says is always right for the moment.* He was ready very early the next day. The dragons had given him dried and salted food which he had put into the harness the previous evening. He also made sure he had the stone, the feather and the cream packed securely. Then he had a huge meal to see him through most of the day.

Favnir had worked out his route with his father and he was prepared for the immediate sea journey. He had to fly in the opposite direction this time. He must travel past Iceland and to a country called Ireland where he was hoping to spend the first night. The following day he was to fly over the south of a country called England and across a small sea to Europe where he could rest overnight. The third day was a long journey over France to Italy where he would rest for the third night. Italy was a long country and he had to travel the length of it to reach the smoking mountain on the fourth day. Then he would meet and probably fight Draakon the tyrant dragon in Italy.

All the dragons came out of the cave. Carlo was waiting outside and he ran over to take his harness from Favnir. He climbed onto the dragon's back and clipped it into position before he sat in it. Favnir saw Elka and Anneka watching and waved one wing.

"I can't wait for this, let's go Flash. I'm ready, I've had a lovely breakfast of fish so my tummy is full." He added as an afterthought, "And I've had a good wee."

Favnir gently flapped his wings to say goodbye and prepared himself. He increased the pressure on his wings and soon they were extended to their full awe inspiring size. He ran a few steps and then he was in the air. He circled round once and dipped one wing in salute, then he headed for Iceland which was a huge island. He flew along the coast of Iceland and then started the flight over the expanse of sea towards Ireland. The sun was till shining and luckily the wind was gentle. He followed his shadow below, it made a welcoming black outline on the water. There was now less ice and it was slightly warmer and for that he was thankful. Carlo had been asleep but now he stirred and sleepily asked where they were. Favnir told him to go to sleep again and rest. Favnir flew on and on for another hour. He was beginning to tire when he saw a welcoming shape on the horizon. He flew lower and knew it was land.

"Time to wake up Carlo. We've found a place to rest." Favnir flew lower and reconnected to his shadow and landed on a pebbly beach. They stayed for an hour during which time they fed on some of the packed food and stretched their legs. There were no humans about and not many animals on the land but Favnir could see seals and he caught a glimpse of a large ugly creature with conspicuously long whiskers that he had never seen before.

As they left this small island Favnir mentally prepared himself for the long journey to reach Ireland. A good three hours flight was in store. He made sure Carlo had his wee and another good stretch and once more they were in the air.

The flight was long and uneventful and when at last they reached land, the sun was setting, the ice was gone and it was much warmer. Hogruth had told Favnir that Ireland was a fertile warm country and had lots of rain, green grass and trees. As Favnir flew over the land he looked down and saw that his father was right. He also saw many humans. He flew higher so he would not be seen so easily. Favnir was looking for somewhere safe to land and eventually he saw a secluded wooded glade below. Carefully he flew lower and made sure there were no humans around. Satisfied, Favnir landed and immediately felt the warmth from the trees. *This will do, time to eat, prepare for tomorrow and sleep.*

# Part Three

# Favnir Pendragon

# Chapter Thirty-Three

## Favnir starts his long journey

Favnir had worked out his route with his father and he was prepared for the next sea journey. He had to fly in the opposite direction this time. He must travel past Iceland and to a country called Ireland where he was hoping to spend the first night. The following day he was to fly over the south of a country called England and across a small sea to Europe where he could again rest overnight. The third day was a long journey over France to Italy where he would spend the third night. Italy was a long country and he had to travel the length of it to reach the smoking mountain on the fourth day. Then he would meet and probably fight Draakon the tyrant dragon in Italy.

All the dragons came out of the cave. Carlo was waiting outside and he ran over to take his harness from Favnir. He climbed onto the dragon's back and clipped it into position before he sat in it. Favnir saw Elka and Anneka watching and waved one wing.

"I can't wait for this, let's go Flash. I'm ready, I've had a lovely breakfast of fish so my tummy is full." He added as an afterthought, "And I've had a good wee."

Favnir gently flapped his wings to say goodbye and prepared himself. He increased the pressure on his wings and soon they were extended to their full awe inspiring size. He ran a few steps and then he was in the air. He circled round once and dipped one wing in salute, then he headed for Iceland which was a huge island. He flew along the coast of Iceland and then started the flight over the expanse of sea towards Ireland. The sun was still shining and luckily the wind was gentle. He followed his shadow below, it made a welcoming black outline on the water. There was now less ice and it was slightly warmer and for that he was thankful. Carlo had been asleep but now he stirred and sleepily asked where they were. Favnir told him to go to sleep again and rest. Favnir flew on and on for another hour. He was beginning to tire when he saw a welcoming shape on the horizon. He flew lower and knew it was land.

"Time to wake up Carlo. We've found a place to rest." Favnir flew lower and reconnected to his shadow and landed on a pebbly beach. They stayed for an hour during which time they fed on some of the packed food and stretched their legs. There were no humans about and not many animals on the land but Favnir could see seals and he caught a glimpse of a large ugly creature with conspicuously long whiskers which he had never seen before.

As they left this small island Favnir mentally prepared himself for the long journey to reach Ireland. A good three hours flight was in store. He made sure Carlo had his wee and another good stretch and once more they were in the air.

The flight was long and uneventful and when at last they reached land, the sun was setting, the ice was gone and it was much warmer. Hogruth had told Favnir that Ireland was a fertile warm country and had lots of rain, green grass and trees. As Favnir flew over the land he looked down and saw that his father was right. He also saw many humans. He flew higher so he would not be seen so easily. Favnir was looking for somewhere safe to land and eventually he saw a secluded wooded glade below. Carefully he flew lower and made sure there were no humans around. Satisfied, Favnir landed and immediately felt the warmth from the trees. *This will do, time to eat, prepare for tomorrow and sleep.*

# Chapter Thirty-four

## Favnir discovers the power of the stone

As he drifted off to sleep Favnir thought about how to avoid being seen by the humans. How could he fly over land and see his shadow and other landmarks to help him navigate and not be seen? He was still thinking about this when he woke the next morning. He still had the harness on his back and told Carlo to take out some dried meat for breakfast. He was once again thankful to the cave dragons for packing the meat in the bag.

"While you are doing that Carlo, can you fetch me the Glittery Stone? I want another close look at it. I have a strange feeling it's hiding some power that we don't know about yet."

Carlo picked up the meat first and threw it down beside Favnir and then carefully took the stone in his mouth and jumped onto the ground. As he did that he tripped on a projecting rock that he hadn't seen and the stone appeared to jump from his mouth. It landed on the rough grass with a clunk and as it did so a fine powdery dust landed on the ground.

"Oh Flash, look at that. That powder came out of the stone as it landed." Favnir was intrigued and crawled over to the dust. He put out his foreleg and rubbed the dust. Carlo shrieked,

"Your arm Flash. It's disappeared. Where's it gone?"

Favnir looked at where his arm should have been and saw nothing. What was most weird was that he could still feel his arm as if it was still there. He heard his mother, *don't panic. You are discovering the stone's power.* He turned to Carlo.

"Keep still Carlo and don't jump about. Now you try rubbing your arm in the powder." Carlo did just that and his paw vanished. Carlo's mouth dropped open and then he was frightened.

"What's happening Flash? This isn't right. That stone seems to be able to make you strong and also make things disappear."

Favnir thought. "Perhaps the stone responds to my mood. Before the fight I was preparing myself for battle and I was fired up inside. But now I was worrying about how to fly and not be seen by the humans and it responded. That stone has magic powers and I think we can make use of them."

"That's good, isn't it Flash? We can become invisible. I wonder how long it will last." Favnir was wondering the same thing.

It was very strange eating food when Favnir's front leg and Carlo's paw had disappeared. But they both said they felt as if their limbs were still there. They ate quickly so they could make an early start. The sun had appeared and the light percolated through the trees to give a beautiful dappled effect in the grove. Favnir decided to risk being seen for a time and only resort to the stone when a lot of humans were around and soon they were in the air flying south east.

The air was now much warmer and Favnir could see lots of trees and valleys. The snow and ice had gone but the wind seemed to be growing stronger. Favnir had been flying for two hours before he saw the sea which separated Ireland from England. According to the sketches which Hogruth had shown him it was only a small sea but it could be very rough. He decided to land and have a rest before he attempted the crossing. There was a lot more dark cloud so Favnir could not see his shadow. This confused him. Finally he saw a suitable sheltered cove by the sea and he managed to land against the strong wind. Carlo slid down from his back quickly and raced away to wee. Favnir looked at the grey sea. Although there was no ice, the never ending waves reached into the air and then turned on themselves to crash down with threatening force. He saw no signs of life in that water.

Both had a quick chew on some dried meat and then Favnir braced himself to fly over this small expanse of sea. In the air he continually scanned the horizon for signs of human activity but saw none. With relief he saw the land mass of England and flew to the coast. The weather had worsened and the clouds looked almost a dark green colour. He heard thunder and he felt Carlo cringe. The thunder got louder and closer and he saw the first signs of lightning. He had to land quickly. He noticed a small human settlement in the distance.

"I'll make for that and hope we can find a spot to land. We must hope that we are not seen."

It started to rain and soon it became a threatening torrent. It landed as hard drops on Carlo's back. He shrieked out in fright. Favnir made for the settlement and flew over it. Luckily no one noticed the outline of an enormous flying creature as people were already in their houses keeping away from the storm. The other side of the village was a wooded area and Favnir landed once again in a grove. They found an overhanging oak tree and huddled together for comfort.

By now the storm had strengthened. The noise of the thunder was deafening and the lightning surrounded them. They watched awe struck when a shaft of lightning hit the tree. It caught fire immediately and Favnir heard the tree's moans of pain and fear.

Favnir worried about his planned journey. It was now mid-morning and he had to fly over England and reach France today. He desperately hoped the storm would weaken soon. The thunder and lightning persisted for an hour before the wind eased. He heard the nearby trees giving sighs of relief. Carlo was still curled into a frightened ball and was hiding under one of Favnir's wings.

"You can come out now Carlo. The storm is passing and we must go soon." Whimpering with misery Carlo slowly emerged. The air was still thick with unfallen rain.

"Can we have something to eat?" Carlo asked tentatively. In answer Favnir reached into the harness and brought out some dried meat which Carlo gulped down.

"The clouds are low and I will have to fly near the ground. It would be best to use the stone and make ourselves invisible. I have a feeling we will be flying over a lot of human settlements."

They shook the stone over the ground and rolled in the powder until every part of their bodies had disappeared.

"Now is the hard part Carlo. You must feel where I am and then work your way into the harness. I don't know how long the effect of this powder will last but I hope it's for a few hours."

Carlo made a big thing of climbing onto Favnir's back. He took so long and obviously thought it was a bit of a joke until Favnir threatened he would leave without him. Quickly he climbed into his harness and Favnir once more soared into the air. The clouds were low and there was no sun, Favnir had no substance and therefore no shadow, which made him feel very alone. Sedna's voice reached into his mind, *Favnir, keep going. You are doing really well.*

Favnir was glad they were invisible as they soon reached many human villages and even larger settlements. Favnir didn't want to stop until he saw the narrow stretch of sea over which he had to fly to reach the main continent. Carlo got more and more restless, he was stiff and ready for a stretch.

"If you don't stop soon Flash, you will have a few very wet scales just about where I am sitting!"

Favnir groaned, he could last a lot longer than Carlo. Then his groans turned into a shout of elation as he saw water on the horizon.

"OK Carlo, we can stop soon. Just hold out a bit longer." Then as he looked at the ground he saw his shadow. He looked at his body and saw his scales shining in the new found sunlight. *I have to find a sheltered place quickly and hope there are no humans around.*

Luck was with him. Soon he was gliding down to a deserted beach which was very close to the water. As soon as the dragon landed Carlo ran off to wee in a bush. Favnir saw that the beach was made of a fine, soft grainy material. It was not rocky and he saw small, rounded hills at the back of the beach. The sea was blue and looked warm and inviting. It was a wonderful place to rest for a short time.

Carlo returned and exclaimed. "Good piece of luck there, Flash. I can see your tail and one wing. It was sheer luck that we found this place in time before we became too visible."

"And I can see your black nose and front paws. I have had Aarja's feather tucked under my neck scale all this time and so far we have been lucky. We can only stay here for half an hour and then we must go. We'll have to use the stone's powder as the effect is beginning to wear off."

Soon they were flying over the narrow sea. Favnir saw countless boats on the water and was really glad that they were invisible. It didn't take long to fly across the sea and the dragon was looking for another beach to rest for the night. It was dusk when he saw the spot he wanted. He circled round before he finally landed. They had reached France. Favnir breathed a huge sigh of relief.

# Chapter Thirty-Five

## Favnir copes without his shadow

The dragon and the fox had reached the mainland but they still had a long journey ahead. Favnir looked for Carlo but all he saw was space and then he heard Carlo's voice calling.

"This is so weird, I can't see you but I know you must be there."

"I'm here alright. Thank Nanuk for the stone. I don't think he meant to help me so much. I'm pretty sure that he didn't know about the invisibility thing." Favnir added, "I think the effect will wear off soon."

But after a couple of minutes Favnir lost contact with Carlo completely. He could no longer hear him. He wondered where he had gone. In fact, Carlo was exploring the top part of the beach. There was scrubland there and he saw some small animals. They had floppy ears and looked quite cute. Then he thought they could make a nice dinner! They were quite unaware of him and they were happily munching at some plants. Carlo leapt on one but it hopped away and looked back in astonishment at the empty space. *OK two can play at that game*, Carlo thought and soon he managed to catch one. He killed it straight away and carried it proudly back to Favnir. They cooked it using Favnir's fire and then it was easy to skin and eat.

While they were eating, parts of their bodies gradually appeared and by the end of the meal they were completely visible. Happily they stretched out and slept.

Favnir was woken up at day break by the sound of human voices. He was instantly alert. The voices seemed to be coming their way. He cautiously stood up and saw two distant figures of human men approaching. They seemed to be carrying long rods and some nets. They were totally engrossed in their conversation and hadn't seen the dragon.

Favnir kicked Carlo and whispered in his ear. "Time to use the stone as quickly as we can. We must go."

Carlo grabbed the stone and shook the powder on the ground. They both rolled in the thick powder and were instantly invisible. Carlo then clambered onto Favnir's back and strapped himself into his harness, placing the stone safely in the pocket as he did so. Soon they were flying through the air to find to find the smoking mountain. Favnir could see many humans and lots of their towns and roads. He decided to follow one of these roads. It seemed to be travelling south in the same direction that he was planning to take. He flew for three hours before he noticed one wing tip was appearing. He was becoming visible and he had to land soon.

Favnir saw a wood ahead to the side of the road. He could see no people and so he landed in a clearing surrounded by trees. Favnir guessed he was out of France and now in Italy. He had to fly another three hours at least to find the mountain. Once more they used the powder from the stone to make themselves invisible and took to the air.

Favnir was finding it hard to cope without his shadow. He felt that part of himself was missing. Again he heard his mother's voice. *You are strong without your shadow. Remember I am always here. You will reconnect with your shadow before you meet the final challenge.*

The dragon was strengthened by Sedna's voice and beat his wings with added energy. Carlo shouted with delight as he felt the surge of air against the dragon's wings.

"Go for it Flash, go faster, go faster."

Favnir was looking for a straight road to follow and soon he found one. As they flew south Favnir felt the warmth of the air against his face and relished it. The sun was getting hotter and hotter. He found he was loving the high temperatures. He looked down and saw many more humans and their towns and roads that led in different directions. Favnir flew for about three hours and when he saw the tip of one wing appearing he decided to find somewhere to land. There was a rocky area ahead and there appeared to be a gorge in the middle of the large rocks.

"Hold on Carlo, I'm going to land. It might be a bit rough." He circled round as he got lower and saw a nice sheltered spot at one side of the gorge. He swooped down and landed very quickly.

Carlo gasped, "I'm so grateful that I'm strapped in. I think I might have been thrown then." He unclipped himself and climbed down still clutching Aarja's feather which he always held lately.

It was obvious to Favnir that Carlo was suffering from the heat. He didn't like it. He was used to the cold snows. Carlo's tongue laid out of his mouth and he was panting hard. His tail was low and his ears were flat. The feather brought them luck again and Favnir saw a stream just behind the cluster of rocks.

"Come on Carlo, there's water here. Let's have a good drink." It was a beautiful clear stream coming from the distant mountains. Carlo leapt over it and head down started drinking. Favnir thought he would never stop. He too needed water and he drank until they were both satisfied. Carlo then leapt into the stream and shrieked out with the shock of icy cold water on his body. The shrieks turned to laughter when he started playing and splashing Favnir with water. The pair needed that play, they both felt better when Carlo eventually climbed out and they settled down to eat.

"That feather certainly brings us luck, Flash."

"Yes, make sure you look after it really well. I think we will need it again when we get to the mountain."

Carlo climbed up to the harness and put the feather in and collected the Glittery Stone. He climbed down and started rubbing his body and part of Favnir's. Gradually their bodies disappeared.

"Now comes the last part of the trek. Another two hours and we should be there. Climb in and let's go."

Once more they were in the air. Favnir guessed he had to fly over the distant mountains to reach his goal. He circled round until he was aiming for the mountains. He noticed that there was much less human activity now and he was thankful for that.

"Hold on Carlo, I am going to fly fast to reach those mountains and I have a feeling that the smoky mountain will be on the other side. Once we have reached the mountains I will slow down."

Carlo clung on and the dragon flew faster than he had ever flown. His enormous wings beat with such power that Carlo couldn't even think let alone speak. As he flew small gusts of fire came from his mouth. It looked weird as his mouth was invisible but Carlo could see the fire. Favnir was letting excess heat escape from his body and it helped him keep cool.

Eventually they reached the mountains. Favnir slowed his speed so he could avoid smashing into some of the rocky crags which reached up into the sky. *This is so different to the snow and ice of Greenland. This is magnificent.* Favnir gazed at the valleys which separated mountains, at the trees which grew to a certain line and then suddenly halted their growth so it appeared as a line of green, above which only the sparse growth of mosses and lichens were seen. At the very top of a few of the highest mountains he could see snow.

Carlo was silent, drinking in the scene.

Favnir slowly flew over this glorious landscape, he didn't want to miss anything. But eventually they flattened out and became hills. On he flew and he realised he was flying down an enormous valley. On the other side he could see more mountains. He fixed his eyes on this range and he thought he saw smoke coiling upwards from one particular point.

"Carlo," he shouted, "do you see smoke coming out of that mountain on the horizon?"

Carlo peered at the peaks in front of them. "Yes, you're right. Do you think that's our mountain?"

"It could well be. I'll look closer when we get nearer."

Favnir flew very slowly towards the mountain. When they were nearly there they both heard deafening rumblings. Favnir's heart gave a jump. *Those are dragon noises. I have found the nest of dragons.*

"That is definitely our smoky mountain. I will look for a place to land in that valley over there. I don't want to get too close until tomorrow."

So Favnir had found the dragon settlement. He landed in a secluded valley near the smoky mountain where they could both rest and prepare for the next day.

## Chapter Thirty-Six

## Favnir challenges the next Cohort member

The dragon thunder woke Favnir at dawn. As he listened he started to pick out different dragon voices. One voice dominated. *That must be the leader, Draakon. Elke said he was really nasty, even worse than Kiddra. He is the one I have to fight and kill.*

He nudged Carlo. "Let's have some breakfast and then we have to make our move." Carlo was soon alert and ready to eat.

"I will take you to the general area of the smoky mountain but you must keep away from the action. You must not be seen, it's too dangerous."

Carlo agreed. He didn't want a repeat of his last experience when he first met Kiddra. Once was quite enough. When they flew this time they had not used the powder. Favnir wanted to be seen. The sun was out and Favnir saw his shadow below. It looked huge and full of power. He locked his vision onto that and feeling much more confident, he soon reached his destination. He landed a short distance away from the peak and Carlo climbed down from his back. Before he did this he rubbed Aarja's feather to collect all the luck he could. He knew Favnir was more in need of both the stone and the feather but he wanted a little bit of luck for himself.

Favnir walked on alone with the harness on his back. As he approached he heard Sedna's voice. *I am with you my son. You are the chosen one and you must use all your willpower to win this fight. Use the stone for strength and invisibility and you will defeat this Dragon and do not forget the feather.*

Favnir got very close to the mountain peak before he was noticed. Favnir was aware of the most massive dragon imaginable standing ahead. He felt fear for the first time and inside he had an urge to turn round and escape. Instead he stood his ground and waited.

The dragon reared up on his hind legs and flapped his massive wings. At the same time, be belched out fire from his mouth, trying to intimidate Favnir. By this time Favnir had noticed three more dragons cowering in the background, watching. The massive dragon turned round to address them.

"Who is this stranger that dares to come to our nest?" He turned back to face Favnir. "How dare you come here? I am Draakon. I am belong to the Cohort group and I am known for my fighting skills and absolute rule. Make yourself known, you puny, little dragon."

Favnir remained on all fours wanting to appear submissive. "I am Favnir from the nest of Vestaris Seamount. I am the Chosen One and am flying the world with a message of Peace. We dragons refute tyranny and war and wish to be at peace with the humans again."

Draakon rose up even higher, furious to hear these words. "How can you challenge me? I have absolute rule here and will not be defied, especially by such a small dragon with those stupid colours. I will fight and kill any who defy me and now I am challenging you. We will meet here in an hour's time when my followers can all watch how I defeat anyone who challenges me."

"I accept that challenge Draakon. In an hour's time then, I will be here."

Because of Draakon's vanity to want all his followers

to watch, Favnir had gained an hour to prepare. He walked back to the spot where he had left Carlo and of course he was there, hiding behind some bushes.

"Carlo, I am fighting Draakon in an hour and haven't much time. I want food first so I have strength. Then I want your help to use the stone's powder. I want to use the power to make my wings and front feet disappear. The effect should last for three hours at least." Favnir had to believe that he would be victor in the coming conflict. He had to believe in himself totally.

As Favnir watched his wings and front feet disappear he remembered his mother's last words and he wiped the feather over his chest and face. It felt strangely comforting. He was ready. He could tell that Carlo was anxious and he gave him a quick hug with his invisible wing.

"I will be back Carlo. After all you have to find Cora again and I have to go back to Elke."

The sun was shining and as Favnir walked back to the Dragon's nest he reconnected with his shadow. He was whole again and although he was nervous he felt confident. He heard Sedna's voice, *I am here Favnir. I am so proud of you.*

There was the Dragon's cave and outside it he saw six onlookers. The dragons were clustered together and they looked weary and uninterested. They had no doubt seen other fights, all with the same result. Draakon had always won and maintained his position of tyranny. Draakon himself was nowhere to be seen. He, no doubt would make his grand entrance when he chose.

Favnir caused a stir of disbelief amongst the dragons. Where were his wings and front feet? He didn't look like a dragon. They could not understand what was going on. Favnir stopped and waited for some time before he heard the expected roaring and thunderous footfall of Draakon the mountain dragon. Draakon made his grand entrance, breathing fire as he came into the open. This was enough to strike fear into the small group of followers who cowered away from him. He wore some protective armour as had Kiddra. It covered his neck and shoulders and Favnir made a mental note of a small joint in the armour between the neck and shoulders which looked vulnerable.

Draakon stopped at the sight of the wingless Favnir. "Is this some trickery?" He roared with anger. "This must be magic and that is not allowed." Favnir still waited motionless as Draakon circled around him.

"I did not know there was a book of rules Draakon. You are wearing armour which I do not have. If you remove your armour then you will see my wings in due course."

Draakon's answer to that was another bellow of anger and an immediate attack onto Favnir's back. Favnir was expecting this and leapt to one side. Favnir had grown to be massively strong but Draakon was still bigger than Favnir. What Draakon had in strength, Favnir had in quickness and agility. Again Draakon pounced, breathing fire, he was aiming at Favnir's underbelly. Favnir felt a burning pain. But then Favnir swiped his invisible wing across Draakon's face which contorted, feeling the hurt. Again and again he did this and he pressed his advantage as Draakon began to feel the pain more intensely. Favnir raised his invisible front foot up to Draakon's face and Favnir's claws felt for his opponents eyes. At the last moment Draakon twisted round and slipped from Favnir's grasp. Draakon darted behind Favnir and trod on his tail securing him in one position. He then breathed fire onto Favnir's exposed back. The pain was agonizing but Favnir kept his head. He managed to twist round and used his other invisible wing to flay Draakon who lost his balance and Favnir's tail was free.

Favnir ultimate aim was to get at Draakon's eyes, but before that he made for the exposed gap in Draakon's armour. Quickly he stretched his neck and blew fire into that gap. Draakon gave out a satisfying moan of pain. Then whilst Favnir had the advantage, his front feet reached for Draakon's exposed eyes. He used his long and dangerous claws to penetrate them. Draakon was shrieking with agony and blood poured from his eye sockets down his face.

"Stop, stop, I concede". But Favnir knew he had to kill his opponent. He breathed fire over every surface of Draakon's body and then looked for Carlo. He knew he would be there watching.

"Kick the stone Carlo" He yelled. Sure enough Carlo was there and he placed the stone on the ground and kicked it with his front foot towards Draakon aiming at his face. The stone hit Draakon's head just above the eyes with a thud. He collapsed in a heap at Favnir's feet.

"I think I would like to rest out here tonight, thank you all the same. Tomorrow we must talk. Perhaps I can come in then?" This was agreed and by the next day Favnir had recovered enough to enter the cave. When asked, Carlo had decided not to go in. He didn't really want to be surrounded by dragons even though they were friendly.

The next day Favnir was taken into the cave by a female dragon. She took him to the male who had spoken to him before.

"I'm Helios. I'm now leader of this group. Welcome."

"I'm Favnir, Protector of the Weak. I have travelled here with my friend Carlo, an Arctic Fox. My father is Hogruth and my mother was Sedna. Now she is a star in the sky but she travels with me and is an unseen companion. I must tell you my story. That will help you understand why we dragons must work together to restore peace in the world amongst the humans."

"I am intrigued. I have all day to listen so go ahead."

Favnir told his story. Helios listened intently and nodded from time to time. When Favnir told him about his human family and how they had helped him he interrupted. "This is wonderful news. I have always thought we should try and interact with humans. I have heard tales that in the past we worked together."

While Favnir was telling his story all the dragons gradually came across to listen. When he finished there was a group sigh of pride in Favnir and what he had achieved.

"I can see what we have to do now," Helios commented. "We must take this gradually but we dragons must extend our territory and humans will in the end accept us again. Then we must try to establish the old relationship between humans and us dragons. But this can't be a sudden change, it has to be gradual."

"Yes, my thoughts exactly. I'll leave you soon to tell Hogruth about the events here. Then I have to fly to Mexico."

"You must rest here for a few days and get your strength back before you travel to Hogruth." So Favnir was rested for a time and soon felt strong enough to journey back. He was approached by Helios who had a suggestion.

"Why don't you take Cidro with you? You intend to fly to Mexico which by all accounts is a long journey. You won't have Carlo with you for the last part and you will need a companion. He is a young strong male. I have asked him and he wants to go with you and learn about the outside world." This took Favnir by surprise. Of course it was a good idea but Helios didn't know about Elke. Favnir had plans to travel with her.

"That seems like a good idea and thank you but it could lead to complications. One thing is that Carlo will almost certainly be jealous and the second thing is that there is a certain female waiting for me at Hogruth's cave and she is probably coming with me." *There I've said it and I want to believe it.*

"I see. That's a pity but I understand. I think Cidro will be disappointed."

Three days passed and then Favnir and Carlo were ready to leave. Favnir decided that he would fly back on the same route using the Glittery Stone's powder to make them both invisible. The time had not yet come to become visible to humans.

The group of dragons stood outside the cave, with Helios in front. Favnir noticed a young male who stood looking at the ground with his head low. *That must be Cidro, I will return and show him the world later.*

The mass of small, dark grey stones scattered as Favnir took to the air, his immense wings creating strong blasts of air. Carlo sat in his harness waving to the dragons below and Favnir dipped his wings in salute. They soon disappeared over the horizon. But Favnir knew he would have to stop when he was over the mountains to use the stone. He was not yet ready to be seen by humans.

## Chapter Thirty-Seven

## The journey back

The journey back to Hogruth's nest was smooth and with no adventures. Again they were invisible and Favnir missed seeing his shadow. He got comfort instead from his inner conviction that his mother was with him. They both felt more relaxed on this return journey and were prepared to just enjoy the flight and the changing scenery. Favnir was wanting to take a bit more time to fly along the coast of Iceland. He was curious about the peculiar whiskered sea creatures he had seen.

Favnir was happy to rest at the same places that they had used before. On the third day they had reached the coast of Iceland and now there was only the final flight to Vestaris Seamount. Favnir flew at a leisurely speed and kept a sharp eye on the huge sea waves.

"There, there's one; no, there are two of them. Do you see them Carlo? They are huge and ugly with their whiskers and tusks."

"Yes, I have a vague memory of my mother telling me about creatures in the sea and I think she talked about an animal called a walrus. I am sure she mentioned that it had big tusks and whiskers."

"That's it then. I'm happy now I know."

Soon they were at the tip of Iceland and veering left for one more flight over the sea to reach Hogruth's island. Both were tired and ready to reach the cave. They were still invisible for the moment but Favnir knew that they would be visible when they flew nearer.

His wing tips were appearing at the moment when he

spied the familiar shape of Vestaris on the horizon. At the same time Carlo screeched with delight as his legs appeared.

"I can see me again, and you, I can see you. Just in time to reach the cave. Wow, haven't we got tales to tell!"

They were both in full view when they reached the edge of Vestaris. They saw dragons appear out of nowhere and gather at the base of the mountain gazing up at the great dragon approaching. As Favnir circled to land he saw frail Hogruth with his older brother and then with a thump of his heart he recognised Elke standing with Anneka, they were positioned to one side.  He landed close to Hogruth and stood still, waiting.

Favnir was weary but his neck was stretched and his head held high. He radiated triumph in his stance. The dragons understood and Hogruth came near.

"Dare I understand that you have succeeded, my son?" Favnir nodded his head and still said nothing. Then Carlo's clear voice was heard coming from Favnir's back.

"Flash is a hero. He was so brave and killed the horrible Draakon dragon. Draakon was much bigger than him but Flash used the stone's powder and killed him. Those dragons are free now."

The dragons crowded round him but Favnir looked only for Elke. She came across and stroked his face. "I am so proud of you Favnir. You are really special to me." Favnir was ecstatic and hardly knew where to look.

Hogruth spoke, "Favnir, you must be tired and weary. Come into the cave and rest. You can tell me all your story. Don't leave anything out."

Carlo slipped down from Favnir's back and crept away by himself but all the dragons including Elke and Anneka went into the cave and heard the tale of how Favnir,

Protector of the Weak, killed the tyrant Draakon. Favnir had killed one more evil dragon, one step nearer freeing the dragon world from their tyranny.

# Chapter Thirty-Eight

## Favnir meets Elke again

It took a long time for Favnir to tell his tale. He wanted to tell the others of the outside world and the wonders he had seen. As he related his tale the tension built up as he neared the climax. Elke kept her gaze on him continually with more and more adoration in her eyes. After the break Favnir continued his tale until he reached the point when he had the fight with Draakon. When he described his fight with Draakon they all leant forward with their mouths open, listening.

They knew about the powers of the Glittery Stone of course but not how much power it had. They learnt too about the good luck feather which Aarja the Arctic Tern had given him.

When Favnir told them about the role Carlo had played, Hogruth looked round the cave. "Where is the fox? I would like to thank him properly."

"I'll try and fetch him but I don't think he will come. He remembers how he was treated by Kiddra and is refusing to come into the cave."

"In that case we will all go outside again." Hogruth painfully got to his feet and slowly made his way out.

Favnir made his way over to the rocks where he knew Carlo was hiding. To his surprise he was joined by Elke. "I will lead you to the place where Carlo hid last time. I know the way well." They found Carlo busy chasing his tail.

"Come back to the cave Carlo. Hogruth wants to thank you for your part in killing Draakon."

Carlo's ears pricked up and he answered. "Well, if you put it like that perhaps I will come to meet the dragons. No funny business though." Elke led the way with Favnir and Carlo following.

The dragons had formed a semi-circle round the cave opening. Hogruth was in the middle and he came forward when he saw Carlo. "Come here little fox. I want to thank you for your bravery. I am sure that Favnir couldn't have defeated Draakon without you."

Carlo visibly swelled with pride. His tail became even bushier and his head was held high. He gave a backward glance at Favnir as if to say, *there, I AM your friend. I always did say so and now it is proven.* Favnir nodded to say that he was with him all the way.

That night Favnir slept outside with Carlo and talked to him about the next stage of their journey. He told him that he was going to ask Elke to come as well. He aimed to fly to the south of Greenland to see Puja and Anana and their family to return the map and tell them their adventures. Then he said he would take Carlo to meet Cora again in the north of Greenland. Then to Mexico to confront the last dragon tyrant and finally back here to Hogruth.

At first Carlo didn't like the thought of taking Elke and Favnir was expecting this. However when he thought about it again he gradually came to accept the idea. After all he was going back to Cora and then Favnir would want a companion.

When Favnir asked Elke if she would fly with him on his journey she looked at him calmly and said. "Favnir, I have been waiting for you to ask me. Of course I will come, I want to be with you to support you now."

Favnir stayed for two more days while he regained his strength for the long trek. He asked Anneka the name of the dragon leader in Mexico. She whispered the name in reply. "His name is Snydervurm." Favnir heard the fear in her voice. "He is a formidable dragon. You will need all the strength and trickery you have to defeat him. He is wily, like a serpent."

After two days the dragons and the fox were ready to go. The harness was fitted and the map, stone, feather, healing balm and food were stowed away. Carlo climbed onto Favnir's back and into his harness. Favnir led the way and Elke followed. Favnir was not expecting to meet many humans so he did not use the stone to become invisible. As Favnir's great wings beat and he circled round to say his goodbye he saw his clear, black shadow below and he heard Sedna's voice. *I do like Elke, my son. But even though you have her, I will travel with you to help you keep safe.* As Favnir flew out to sea he looked back and saw the familiar flat top of the ancient volcano and wondered if he would ever see it again.

# Chapter Thirty-Nine

## Carlo thinks of a plan

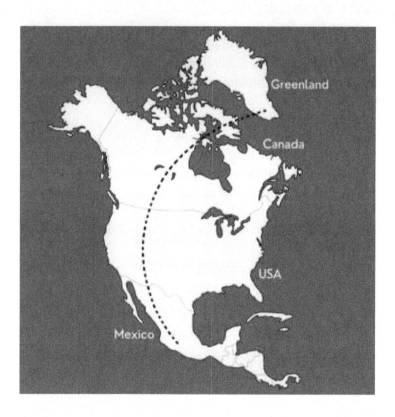

First they had to fly over the Greenland Sea to reach Sydkap. Elke flew behind Favnir and was sheltered in the wake of Favnir's wings. This time the weather elements seemed to work against them. The sky darkened and the wind raged. It blew into his face and into the sea below. The sea water lashed onto the ice floes and Favnir could see seals huddled together on the ice. As he watched he saw one massive wave fall on one floe and sweep a group of seals into the sea. He watched a killer whale approach and then more swirling of the water, blood, and no more seals. Favnir flew on. He was aware of Elke close behind. Carlo for the most part was quiet but Favnir heard the occasional moan of terror. Then he felt torrents of rain coming from the black clouds and he knew they had to find an island to land. Favnir desperately searched the horizon and then he heard a shout from Carlo.

"There's an island, slightly to the left." Favnir looked and saw land. With relief he aimed for it and landed on a beach where he could see caves. Caves would do, both to dry off and eat.

"Luck again," Carlo exclaimed," I was rubbing Aarja's feather. Don't worry, it's still safe."

Gentle flames from the dragon's mouths both warmed and dried them and soon they were eating. Elke looked at Favnir and spoke very calmly. "Well, Favnir that was exciting. But you did so well and guided us both magnificently."

Carlo interrupted indignantly, "Hang on, I saw this island don't forget. I have sharper eyes than Flash."

"Yes, I know you did, I'm sorry. You did well there Carlo."

"And another thing, let's get this straight. I'm his best friend and I call him Flash. When we reach our human family you will see that they call him Flash as well. So you had better get used to it."

Favnir had gone to the cave mouth and diplomatically interrupted. "Hey, the rain has stopped and the sky is much lighter. I think we can go soon. We still have a good hour's flight to the mainland."

Outside the rain had stopped and the wind had dropped but the heavy clouds were still in the sky. No sun, no shadow. Favnir felt disquiet but they had to continue their journey. They flew for two hours without any incident and finally Favnir saw Sydkap lying ahead. He wanted to land before they reached the settlement and rest for the night. Favnir saw the place they had used before and made for that. It was late afternoon and the light was fading rapidly. The two dragons landed and Carlo slid off Favnir's back and disappeared behind some nearby bushes. It was icy cold and Carlo was shivering and his fur was standing up. The two dragons blew small balls of fire and Carlo stood near.

They rested overnight until dawn came. Using the stone powder they made themselves invisible which was a new experience for Elke but as usual she took it calmly.

"OK, let's go." Favnir was eager to start. He was aware of the long distances he would have to cover before he reached the humans. Carlo was behaving in a strange way, rather like the time before when he had confessed to Favnir that he had seen his mother. His tail and ears were down and he was taking two steps forward and one back as he made his way to Favnir. Something was bothering him.

"Flash, do you think it might be a good idea if you left me with Cora before you meet Puja and the others? It's on the way, isn't it? It seems silly to go to the humans first and come up here again for me and then go down to the coast again to fly to Mexico. I would like to see the humans but you are their friend not me."

Favnir thought and said. "You are right, it would make more sense. If that's OK with you that's what we will do." Inside he thought, *I really hope Cora is still around. Carlo will be really upset if she has found another friend while he's been away.*

# Chapter Forty

## Parting of the friendship

The more Favnir thought about Carlo's plan the more it made sense. If Carlo wanted to team up with Cora then so be it. But it did make him sad. They had been friends for such a long time and Carlo had helped him out of many tight corners. The fox could be very annoying and of course in the past had lied to him but that was over and he didn't want to lose him. But he had Elke now and his new life was starting. Favnir had thought Carlo would have wanted to meet Puja and her family again to say goodbye properly but after all, they were his friends and not Carlo's.

Favnir and Elke flew for nearly two hours before they started becoming visible again. That was when Favnir heard Carlo's excited shrieks.

"There's the place Flash. I would recognise it anywhere." At once Favnir recognised the flat valley surrounded by trees where Carlo had met Cora. Favnir turned a little to the left and circled round to find a good place to land. The sun was shining through the intermittent clouds and he saw his shadow. Again the presence of his shadow gave him confidence and he reconnected with it on landing. Almost immediately Elke followed and they were both on the snowy surface.

Carlo couldn't wait to find Cora. He darted to the trees and shouted at the top of his voice. "Cora, I'm here. I've come back for you." Cora did not appear. Carlo frantically darted backward and forward, circling round and round shouting for his friend. No Cora.

*Where was she?* Carlo was now frantic with worry.

Favnir said, "Come and sit down Carlo. I expect she will turn up soon. Come and have some food." Carlo sat down but couldn't settle. In the end he jumped to his four legs and darted off again shouting out, "I'm going to look again. I know she's somewhere near."

Favnir and Elke finished eating. "I had better go and help Carlo look for Cora. Perhaps if I flew over the area I would stand a better chance of spotting her. Can you could hang on here and then if Carlo comes back he won't think we have left him."

Elke agreed to this and Favnir took to the air. He circled round slowly in ever increasing circles. He saw Carlo below him frantically looking in every unlikely spot. Carlo saw Favnir and waved his front paw.

Then Favnir saw something in the woods. He saw the fallen tree first and then a tangled mass of branches and then, he saw a fox caught in the mass of fallen shrubbery. The fox was alive but trapped in the undergrowth. It was struggling and trying to get free. Then Favnir saw the brown patches on the shoulders and knew it was Cora. He sighed with relief. He couldn't bear to think of how upset Carlo would be if Cora had been killed or if she had gone missing. He back tracked to where he had last seen Carlo and flew low to shout down to him.

"Found her. Cora is alive but she's caught in the branches of a fallen tree. I can't land here but I will fly slowly so you can follow me."

Cora was whimpering with fear when Carlo found her but her eyes flickered with happiness when she saw him.

"I can't move," she whispered.

"Don't worry, we'll soon get you out of this. Flash will help, I know."

"Stay with her," Favnir shouted. "I'm going back to tell

Elke to come here." Soon both dragons were back. They hatched a plan between them. First they carefully blew fire in the area around the trapped fox and then they landed on the burnt ground. Having cleared that area they could move nearer to Cora. With their immense combined strength they succeeded in pushing and pulling the fallen branches away from the ensnared fox. When they had removed all the heavy branches only a few long twigs were trapping Cora. Carlo then bit his way through these and at last Cora was free.

"It all happened so quickly," she explained. There was a storm and the lightning struck a tree and it fell on me. I could do nothing and I have been trapped there all last night and this morning. I am so thirsty."

Carlo interrupted, "I saw a stream on the way here and it looked good for drinking. Let me take Cora and you two can catch up with us there. We can all have a drink." That sounded like a good idea and Carlo and Cora ran off together.

Elke looked at Favnir and said, "They look really good together. They will probably have lots of fox cubs and then Carlo will be busy." They waited for a bit and then slowly flew in the same direction that the two foxes had taken. They easily spotted them, drinking from a gently flowing stream. There was luckily, a clear patch nearby and the two dragons landed easily. They too were in need of a drink.

But far too soon Favnir knew it was time to leave. He found it difficult to believe that he would be leaving his friend and he would have to go on his big adventure without him.

"Carlo, we must go. I will take your harness with me and everything that is in it. I have a nasty feeling that I will need the Glittery Stone and the lucky feather and even the healing balm before I finish."

"Don't forget me Flash, never forget me. Come back and see me soon."

"Of course I will, you silly fox." Carlo rubbed his bottom along Favnir's leg and then, when Favnir knelt down, went to his head and stroked his face. Favnir felt those mysterious drops of water in his eyes. "Look after him," he said to Cora.

Carlo called to Elke, "you look out for Flash. If danger comes near, be there for him. He needs looking after sometimes." Favnir couldn't stop any longer. He flapped his wings and soon the two dragons were in the air.

Their destination this time? To find Favnir's human family.

# Chapter Forty-One

## Favnir searches for his human family

Favnir couldn't make sense of his thoughts. So many things were pounding through his mind. For one thing, the sky was grey with heavy cloud and he could not connect with his shadow. The second thing was that he was really upset at leaving Carlo. The third thing was the worry of meeting Puja and her family again. He had grown so much since he had last seen them. He was fretting about how they would feel when they met again. The fourth thing was of course, his happy turn of events in having Elke always with him. That was not a worry at all. When he thought of that, he felt joyful and content. He flew on, very slightly ahead of Elke so he could take the lead.

The two dragons flew on over the snow covered landscape. The bitterly cold air tried to freeze their breaths but sporadic flames from their mouths prevented this happening. The sun appeared sometimes through broken cloud but not enough to see Favnir's shadow clearly. Favnir knew the mountains lay ahead and wanted to land safely before they reached them.

Elke was beginning to tire a little when Favnir saw the slopes on the horizon. "OK, there are the mountains. I will look for a place to land." Almost immediately he saw an ideal spot and guided Elke down to land on soft snow. They were hungry for some meat from their supply and ate it quickly.

"When do we use the stone again?" Elke asked.

"Not yet, there won't be many humans around. Perhaps when we have flown over the mountains, the next stage is going to be hard and take a long time. But I will rub the feather for luck."

Soon they were in the air again and heading for the mountains. Favnir shuddered when they reached the spot where Carlo had fallen into the crevice. He pointed his wing at the place and called out to Elke.

"That's where Carlo fell, I don't want to think about that. But of course that's also where he found the Glittery Stone. Everything happens for a purpose I suppose." On and on they flew. Favnir knew he had to reach his mother's cairn and show it to Elke. They would rest there.

Favnir smelt the sea. The scent brought back so many

memories such as Carlo sniffing the air and telling Favnir the story of how his mother had told him about salt and the sea. Favnir saw the pile of stones in the distance.

He shouted to Elke. "There's the cairn where my mother is resting. We'll stop there for a while." Favnir circled round and carefully landed in his chosen spot very near the cairn. Elke kept back, as always she could feel that Favnir wanted to be alone. Favnir placed his front claw on the stones and stayed motionless. He felt vibrations coming through the stones and then he heard a voice. *You have done so well my son. You are full of power now and proving that you are the Chosen One. Keep strong and I will come with you this one last time to fight Snydervurm. He is the last of the Cohort.*

Favnir took his claw away from the stones. Soon the two dragons were in the air again flying northwest to find Favnir's human family. Again they flew over familiar land to Favnir and he pointed out the spot where he had hatched and Carlo had offered his friendship.

Favnir knew the humans must be fairly close and he carefully watched the landscape for signs. He saw the igloos first and gave an excited gasp. As he approached he saw humans looking at the sky. They had seen the dragons. The sun was shining and he saw his shadow clear cut and black below him. Favnir reconnected with it and landed.

He heard a shriek of recognition. Puja was running full pelt to meet him. Aka was not far behind. Behind them Anana was standing with a smile on her beautiful face but then she suddenly stopped and Favnir saw the pleasure on her face replaced by puzzlement. "Where's Carlo?" she asked and "Who is this?" She pointed at Elke who had landed some distance away.

"That's Elke who is my friend. She is flying with me at

the moment." I'll tell you all about it later and then I will explain about Carlo." When her face showed her concern he added, "He's fine, but he has met a female friend called Cora. He sends his love."

Favnir walked on to Anana. "I am back as I promised, to bring you the map. I made good use of it and I've also got the healing cream. If I can, I will keep some of the cream, I have a feeling I will need it on this next journey. I will also keep Carlo's harness as it's wonderful for carrying the Glittery Stone and feather and the balm of course."

"Keep the harness and the cream. When you come back you can leave the harness with us. Perhaps in the future Carlo and you will come and see us and then he might need the harness anyway."

Elke was following slowly and keeping back all the time. She, of course didn't understand or speak the human language, so she didn't really know what was going on. They stayed two nights with the humans regaining their strength for the tortuous flight ahead. During that time Elke formed a friendship with the humans and Anana showed her how she baked her bread.

On the third day they departed as soon as the sun was up. Favnir said an emotional goodbye and made a promise to return as soon as he could.

# Chapter Forty-Two

## Hope seen in a sunset

Favnir wanted to fly to South Greenland to a place called Cape Farewell. Kiuvuk had told him to expect high mountains in that area. After that it would be a very long flight across the ocean to Canada. He thought it would be best for them to be invisible for most of the flight as there were going to be more ships around carrying lots of humans.

Elke's calming presence was a huge support to Favnir. She was so different to Carlo who was always so excitable. But he also missed feeling Carlo on his back. After two hours they landed for a rest and Elke looked for the stone in the harness. She held it in her mouth and shook it onto the ground and they both rolled in the powder.

"Wow!" Elke exclaimed. "This is really weird. All I can see of us is the Glittery Stone. I had better put it back into the harness before we lose it."

"Don't even talk about that. We must never lose it. We don't want to be seen by the humans yet and I'm pretty sure I will need it for fighting Snydervurm."

Soon they were in the air flying south to the sea. They flew over flat valleys where they saw some scattered human settlements. Favnir saw scrubby patches of dwarf spruce and birch, growing in defiance of the snow. There were rocks showing signs of surface green growth. These were the lichens and mosses.

As they flew further south the flat terrain disappeared to be replaced by hills. Huge crags of jagged rocks appeared with ice cold lakes filling hollows in the ground.

It was bitterly cold and Favnir wished he had Carlo's coat of fur which he could make stand upright to keep him warm. The jagged rocks disappeared and were replaced with huge mountains. The tree line was low down and the peaks were white with snow and ice. The lakes were still present, clear as crystal and a pure, deep blue competing with the blue of the sky.

Then the sun started to sink and Favnir knew he had to find a place to land. He was approaching the headland of Egger Island and he could see a large settlement ahead which could only be Cape Farewell. Elke came close and he felt her presence, then he heard her voice.

"Look to the left Favnir." He looked and saw a small lake with a flat area surrounding it. It was protected by small rocks. He veered left and circled before landing. His wings were becoming visible and he could see Elke's tail so they were just in time.

As their bodies showed themselves so did the sky light up with the colours of sunset. The sun was low on the horizon and disappearing with every second. Streaks of indigo, orange and red flashed across the sky until Favnir felt overcome by the colour changes. Then green became the main colour and Favnir saw that green light dancing in the sky which itself was dark navy blue. The contrast was indescribable. He glanced at Elke and saw she too was transfixed, staring at the display in the sky. Then it was over, the sun had sunk for the night. The moon appeared and gave them some light to see so they could eat before they rested.

When Favnir woke at dawn he saw that Elke was already on her feet exploring the area. She was inspecting the nearby rocks with their layers of moss and lichens. Their colour showed a triumph of life appearing above the snow. She turned to see Favnir standing near.

"Look at this greenness Favnir. Isn't it wonderful? It gives me hope." Favnir came to her and they stood wing to wing for a bit. Then together they prepared for the flight.

Elke took the Glittery Stone and shook it. They rolled in the powder as before until they had disappeared. The sun was in the sky by then and Favnir saw it was going to be a clear day. They took to the air and then saw the sea.

This was the edge of the Labrador Sea, an arm of the Atlantic Ocean. To Favnir it appeared cruelly cold. The packed ice mostly hid the water. Favnir was aiming for an island called Newfoundland just off the coast of Labrador in Canada.

Favnir saw a few seals resting on the ice and later when they were well into their flight he saw a couple of whales in more open water. The flight was long and although they were both fit and full of power, after flying for nearly two hours they were beginning to tire. He saw a small island at last and thankfully flew down to land.

There were birds around and one Osprey almost collided with him and another bumped into Elke's wing. Favnir saw the bird give a jump of astonishment when it met with a mass of hard scales in the midst of clear air!

The spot Favnir found was ideal to rest and think about his planned journey. Anneka had told him how far he had to travel. He knew they would have to fly about 4000 miles and he had allowed twelve days to do this. He was hoping to have two days to recover once they had arrived, before he accosted Snydervurm. Then they would have to fly over the huge countries of Canada and America to the border with Mexico. The inactive volcano they sought was in an area called the Pinacate Peaks.

By the time they had rested properly they were

becoming visible again. Elke once again shook the stone to see the thick, yellow powder. They rolled in it and once again they were invisible. Sedna's voice sounded in his head, *Courage, my son. The future of the dragons is with you. I am still with you and we will be partners. Elke is wonderful for you, she is so calm and will give you the courage you need.* As they took flight, even though they were invisible, Favnir could just make out his shadow on the ground and then on the sea. It was blurred and indistinct but it was there.

# Chapter Forty-Three

## At last the dragons find Snydervurm

The next twelve days were a revealing and new experience for Favnir. He loved having Elke with him, she was always such a calming influence and that stopped him worrying too much. She was convinced that he was the Chosen One and supported him all the way. Using the stone's powder they remained invisible but he saw how the humans were taking over the world. They passed over huge towns and saw the roads they had built and he saw the smoke that was pouring out of their factory chimneys. In the forests he saw how some people hunted the animals and he shuddered when he saw that they were doing it for sheer enjoyment. He watched with horror one day when he saw a magnificent moose shot and the man held the head up with triumph while the other man pointed a box like thing at him and clicked something. Favnir didn't understand what that was but he did understand the sheer senselessness of what the man had done.

They both had to maintain top speed to complete the mileage for each day and they had to find somewhere to recover. They flew across Canada and down through America and knew they were nearing their destination when they reached Arizona State. Mexico was next and the Pinacate Peaks were in the north.

When they arrived at the Peaks their tails and heads were drooping and their scales were dull and lusterless. What worried Favnir most was they couldn't breathe fire. They didn't seem to have enough energy to produce that dragon life force. They had to find isolation somewhere to rest for two days before they went on to find Snydervurm. Favnir was in no state to walk far, let alone fight. Luckily they still had a supply of food for the next few days.

Favnir knew why this area was called the Peaks. It was a magnificent awe inspiring mountainous area with scrubby vegetation. There were pathways on which humans walked for pleasure so Favnir searched for a secluded small valley between mountains and away from any paths. He circled in the air and at last found a lovely space between two mountains. Before they landed Favnir saw his shadow. When he reconnected he felt strength and optimism returning.

They spent two days together and got to know each other. At the end of the two days Favnir was convinced he had found his life partner, Elke was loving and supportive, calm and courageous. On the third day Favnir woke early and stretched himself before walking to the nearby stream to drink. He jumped a little with happiness as he was walking and realised fire was escaping from his mouth. "I knew it would come back," he shouted to Elke. "Come over here and have a drink. Try your fire skills too."

Favnir saw Elke produce her fire and realised that both of them were ready now for the challenge of meeting Snydervurm. He still hoped to negotiate but deep down he knew he would have to fight the tyrant.

Anneka had given him the idea that the smoking mountain was about an hour's flight from the border with Mexico. They would have to fly west over the inactive mountains to find smoke and perhaps hear 'thunder'. They rolled in the stone's powder to make themselves invisible and took to the air again. As they flew they drank in the warmth. No snow here only the glorious heat from the sun. Favnir saw the cedars and birch trees growing on the base of the mountains, then the green colour coming abruptly to an end and being replaced by the dark grey rock.

Elke saw it first, "Look, over to the right." Favnir turned his head and saw a faint coil of smoke on the horizon.

"Yes, I see it." They both dipped their right wings and turned in the direction of the smoke. As they got closer they could hear the familiar dragon 'thunder', the overpowering cacophony of the sounds of a dragon's nest. "We've got here at last. Let's find a safe place to land and meet them tomorrow. I need to get into my fighting mood to meet Snydervurm."

# Chapter Forty-Four

## Favnir uses the stone's power

They soon found a secluded valley in between the smoking mountain and another nearby hill. Tired out, the dragons watched their solid forms reappear. Elke went exploring and found a lovely bubbling stream where they drank to their full. Although they felt more normal after their drink, Favnir just wanted to rest and think about his fight strategy for the next day. He had no doubt that it would come to that, another fight to the death.

The next day the sky was dark and full of threat, and the very air Favnir breathed seemed filled with dangers to come. His shadow was not with him and Favnir shuddered but then he heard Sedna's voice. *Forget your fears Favnir, you know you can win. I am with you all the way.* He drew himself more upright so he felt taller and looked at Elke.

"We both need to eat, we need energy. Then we must go to the Nest of Dragons."

Elke spoke.

"You are the Chosen One and I know that you will defeat Snydervurm. Don't forget the feather."

Favnir couldn't believe that he had momentarily forgotten his lucky feather. How could he have done this? He thought of that tiny bird who had given him her feather for luck. Elke took it out of the harness and Favnir rubbed the feather against his chest. Now he felt his luck returning. He put it safely under his neck scale.

Now they could hear the thunderous dragon voices and they flew towards the noise. They were seen before they landed and when they did, they were met by four dragons who all wanted to know who they were and where they had come from. Favnir didn't have time to reply because another dragon appeared at the mouth of the cave. The atmosphere changed and he immediately took charge. He came over to Favnir and Elke, the other dragons all fell back.

"Hello there, you look as if you have travelled a long way, you must be very tired. You look weary and in need of rest." His voice was oily and smooth. Favnir felt himself being overcome by his hypnotic speech. "Come into the cave and we can talk more." Favnir saw Elke shake her head slightly. "I am Snydervurm, and you are?"

Snydervurm wasn't what Favnir had expected. He was shorter than Favnir with tiny wings and tail. His body was almost black. His eyes were small and beady but with a sharp intelligence in them. His voice was charismatic and musical. Sedna's inner voice came to him. *On no account go into the cave. Do not believe his soft voice.*

"I am Favnir and Hogruth is my father and Sedna my mother. I have come a long way to see you. I have met Anneka who lived here but who left your nest. This is Elke who is a friend of Anneka. She also doesn't like any form of tyranny. I am trying to rid the world of dragon despots. We must reestablish friendly relationships with the humans." Snydervurm replied.

"Yes, it was a pity about Anneka, I always thought she was a lovely dragon. I tell you what, I will consider your plan to be friends with humans if you accept my leadership and join my group. How is that for an offer?"

"No way will I do that. I am going back to my father's nest on Vestaris Seamount. Dragons have to work together and not have one despotic overriding leader."

Snydervurm's eyes flared with a terrible anger at what

Favnir said. He shook with fury as his voice changed and he threw out his challenge. "In that case you leave me no choice but to challenge you to a fight. One more chance to live, you stupid upstart. If you don't take that back you will not live another day. Come back here at sunset and we will settle this for once and all." He swung round showing his sleek and muscular body and went back into his cave. The other dragons followed.

Favnir and Elke flew back to their quiet spot to spend five hours waiting for sunset. The sky was still covered in dark grey clouds but the sun could be seen peeping through little gaps in the cloud cover. Who would win this battle, the sun or the clouds? Favnir felt it was an omen. He watched the sky intently. The gaps in the clouds grew larger and the sun shone more brightly, eventually, soon after midday the sky was azure blue and the sun shone. Favnir could see his shadow again.

Something told him that this was to be a harder battle than the other two. Snydervurm was smaller certainly but he had an intelligent cunning which Favnir would have to penetrate.

He suddenly said to Elke. "Make sure you have the stone with you and keep it handy." He remembered how useful the stone had been in his other two fights. He couldn't be without the stone nearby. He had the feather in his claw and he stroked it from time to time.

When the sun was low on the horizon they flew to the smoking mountain again. They landed near the cave and waited. Nine dragons were there around the cave mouth and then Snydervurm almost danced out, his black scales shimmering in the setting sun and reflecting a reddish colour which gave him a sinister appearance. He felt no need for any protecting armour. Favnir stood motionless and waited for Snydervurm to begin his moves.

As Snydervurm danced around Favnir he kept prodding him with his front leg. His dances quickened and he started taunting him about his coloured stripes and then he started insulting his mother.

"Your mother must have been so ugly if she gave you those terrible stripes. She must have been stupid as well to have dropped you as an egg in Greenland of all places." He had obviously done some research and talked to a dragon who had been in touch with Anneka.

That was hard to take and Favnir found himself losing control. He heard his mother's voice. *Take no notice*

*Favnir. Snydervurm is trying to wind you up.* He heard Elke's voice as well in the real world telling him to stay calm.

Snydervurm gradually increased the tempo of his dancing and circled round Favnir quicker and quicker until Favnir felt dizzy trying to keep track of Snydervurm's position. Suddenly Snydervurm lunged forward with his mouth wide open and aimed for Favnir's neck. At the same time he blew fire from his mouth. At the last moment Favnir dodged and escaped. Now Favnir swiftly turned and aimed a blow at Snydervurm's back with his massive front leg. If it had connected, Snydervurm would have been disabled but it didn't. Snydervurm reacted too quickly for the blow to land. Again Snydervurm saw an opening in Favnir's defense and emitted a massive flame aiming at Favnir's neck. This time Favnir felt a terrible pain and crumbled to the ground. Then Snydervurm leapt forward and aimed fire at Favnir's wings. Favnir felt he had failed and lost this fight.

He heard Elke shouting, "Look over here." Favnir looked to see the Stone in Elke's mouth. She spat it towards him, giving it a shake. Favnir used all the strength he had left and dived into the dust. There were gasps from the watching dragons when Favnir vanished. Snydervurm gave a roar of anger which turned into a moan of pain when Favnir crawled under Snydervurm's belly and blew fire onto his underside. Favnir followed this with bite after bite. Blood poured from Snydervurm's body and Favnir turned his attention to his neck. More bites followed until Snydervurm fell to the ground. But he refused to die quickly.

"You used magic to win. Where did you get that magic? This was an unfair contest, I should have won." Having spoken those words Snydervurm died. Favnir had defeated the last evil dragon.

# Chapter Forty-Five

## Elke proves herself

Favnir had won the fight but he was left terribly injured and in dreadful pain. He collapsed onto the ground and groaned in agony. The pain was like a sharp knife tearing at his neck and wings. He was beginning to be visible again as there had only been a small cloud of powder and Elke rushed over in an unusual panic and bent down over his face. He managed to say between his gasps. "Fetch the healing cream."

She hurriedly fetched the cream from the harness and by the time she reached Favnir she had returned to her usual calm. With her front claw retracted she smoothed the cream onto Favnir's neck and the tips of his wings. Within a few minutes Favnir had stopped writhing and moaning.

"Keep the cream safe, I will need it again soon. Put it back into the harness and keep the harness with you."

Elke suddenly realised she had forgotten the stone. She glanced back to where it should have been but could not see it. Again she felt an unfamiliar feeling of panic. The she saw a group of three young dragons grouped together and obviously looking at something. She edged closer and peered through their wings. They had the stone and were passing it from one to the other, obviously very curious about how it had produced the powder.

"Please, can I have the stone back?" She decided to tell them the truth. "Favnir was given it by the Polar Bear God Nanuk, in Greenland. It was to keep him safe because Nanuk wanted his Power when he was fully grown. So you see it is important that he keeps it, for the moment anyway."

They were shaking it roughly to try to get the powder out but it wasn't working. "It works only for Favnir or anyone who is helping him. It won't work for you."

At last they gave it back to Elke who put it into the harness together with the cream.

Favnir had managed to stand by the time she had returned but it was obvious that he was incapable of flying. One female dragon stepped forward and offered to help him recover in their cave. Elke decided she was trustworthy and nodded her head. It appeared that the female dragon had taken charge. She gave orders to the others who appeared to want to help Favnir. But both Favnir and Elke noticed two males at the back of the group who were muttering to each other and looked rather rebellious. They had been part of the group who had taken the stone.

It took three days for Favnir to fully recover with the help of Anana's healing cream. They were treated well by the group. Favnir was told about an underground stream which flowed through the deeper parts of the cave from which they took their water. He felt a strange urge to discover it. On the last day of his recovery he found it. As he leant over the clear inky blue water he saw his mother. She was looking up at him and said nothing but her face was full of love and pride. Favnir kept this image to himself and didn't tell anyone, not even Elke.

They left on the fourth day just after dawn. By now Favnir had told them all his story and they knew their destiny was to gradually contact humans and interact with them. Even the two young rebellious dragons came round to accept this. But there was something else that Favnir wanted to tell Elke.

"Elke, I must tell you about Nanuk, the Polar Bear God. He told me about the Glittery Stone and I know he will want it back. I must be prepared to meet him fairly soon."

"Aren't you worried about what he might want to do to you when he gets the stone in his massive paws?"

"I am a little apprehensive but I am so powerful now. I think I will be able to defend myself."

Elke's mouth turned down and she looked the other way.

The female leader gave them a massive pack of food to last them until they had reached Greenland.

This time they were more prepared for the long journey. They flew steadily back along the same route and Favnir connected with his shadow as often as he could. They soon left Mexico and then flew through Arizona and up through America to Canada, across Canada and onto Newfoundland. Ten days passed before they had found Cape St Francis. Then came the long sea crossing over the Labrador Sea to reach Greenland where they landed on Egger Island again for a well-deserved rest. Then they flew north to find Puja and her family.

It was strange to see the cold snowy landscape of Greenland again. Yet this was what Favnir was born into and he felt strangely at home. He still didn't really like the cold air but he accepted this as part of his life. Now they did not use the powder to be invisible. They flew high and were not seen by the few humans. On and on they flew until they felt weary. Favnir had to admit to himself that he was really worried about returning the Glittery Stone to Nanuk. They were in a mountainous landscape and Favnir found a valley in which to land.

"We should keep here for the night and tomorrow we should reach the human settlement."

Elke agreed by nodding her head. But then she exclaimed, "What's happening Favnir?"

A thick mist had descended upon them and they could no longer see one another. It was becoming denser by the second. Around the edges it blurred into purple. Favnir knew what was coming and he began to shake with fear. This was bringing back early memories. The edges of the mist started to form a shape and it was the shape of Nanuk the Polar Bear God. A voice thundered out from the cloud,

"We meet again Favnir. I hardly recognise you. You are now a magnificent dragon." Nanuk saw Favnir give a start of surprise. "Yes, I know your true name. You will now return the stone to me, you have no further use for it."

Favnir made himself stop shaking and glanced sideways at Elke who was transfixed. Favnir prodded her with his front claw to rouse her from her trance.

"Elke, can you reach inside the harness and lift the stone out of its pocket. Then give it to me."

Favnir in turn passed it over to Nanuk who reached out to grab it from Favnir. Nanuk then moved very close to Favnir and laughed in his face.

"Ha, you stupid dragon. You have fallen into my trap. This stone contains my essence and now no one can harm me. Now I will draw out your power."

"No you will not Nanuk. I am now fully grown and I have defeated the Cohort of Dragons. It is time now to defeat you."

Elke watched as Favnir blew his awe inspiring flame towards Nanuk and waited for the Bear God to yell in pain. Nothing happened. The flame seemed to disappear into space and had no effect. Favnir blew another and another and all of them did not even reach Nanuk.

"You can't harm me Favnir. While the Glittery Stone is

near me nothing can do me harm. I am safe."

Elke watched in horror as Nanuk leapt towards Favnir. Favnir tried to escape but Nanuk caught his left wing and

pulled him down. Favnir tried to defend himself with bites and scratches as well as flames and nothing worked. Elke now decided to join in and blew flames onto Nanuk. Again there was no effect. Now Nanuk bit Favnir's throat. In disbelief Elke watched as a purple smoke emerged from Favnir's mouth. Nanuk took deep breaths as he started inhaling the smoke and then he grew bigger and bigger as he continually inhaled it.

Elke now looked at Favnir and saw his coloured stripes fading until his skin looked as pale as the surrounding snow. Nanuk laughed at Elke as she tried futilely to blow fire onto Nanuk. Nanuk laughed back at her.

In desperation Elke twisted her neck around hoping for some inspiration. She saw the Glittery Stone lying on the snow near Nanuk and pounced on it. Inspiration came suddenly, she nerved herself to come close to Nanuk and shoved the stone into his mouth and closed his jaws around it. That at least stopped Nanuk from breathing in more of Favnir's smoke. She continued to push at the stone. Suddenly an earth splitting crack was heard coming from Nanuk's mouth. The stone had split.

Fascinated Elke watched as Nanuk turned orange then an amber colour. Finally as he shrunk to the size of Carlo, sparks appeared on his body and at the very end he disappeared. Elke saw another Glittery Stone lying in Nanuk's place. He had become a Glittery Stone. Nanuk had gone forever. Elke looked at Favnir who still lay on the snow but saw his purple stripes gradually returning.

Elke knew there would be no more flying today. Favnir would have to rest at least a week before he had recovered his strength for the rest of the journey.

He remained unconscious until the next day and for the next week Elke tended Favnir's every need until he felt well enough to fly. He didn't fully recover all his power for many months. But he knew he had to see his human family before he returned to his father's nest.

# Chapter Forty-Six

## Anana heals Favnir

Favnir had to find the humans. He knew that Puja would be worried about him. He was very late for his return. Favnir desperately wanted to leave that place where he had met Nanuk and now they were in the air. They retraced their original flight and a few hours later they saw the settlement. He heard excited shrieks coming from the ground and of course there was Puja watching the sky. She was alone but soon Anana and Aki had joined her.

Favnir circled around and when he had seen his clear shadow he connected with it on the ground. Elke followed and landed close by. Puja rushed forward and hugged his wing and neck where she saw the remains of his injuries.

"You have been wounded badly. Those marks are still open to the air and look sore. How did you get them?"

"That's a long story Puja. Let's leave it for later. I'm so happy to be here, there have been times when I thought I never would see you again. I just want to rest for a few days."

Anana spoke. "Shall we go to the igloo and I will find some more healing cream and treat those wounds. You must be hungry, I will find some food for you both." She looked at Elke. "Come with us, you are very welcome. You must be tired and hungry as well." Placid as always Elke nodded and followed them to the igloo.

Kiuvuk was waiting. He had seen them and he had been preparing some food and drinks. His face lit up when he saw Favnir again. "Hi, glad you're back Favnir, you look half starved. Here's some food ready and waiting. We'll all eat outside."

Anana intervened, "Before we eat I must treat Favnir's wounds." She went into the tent and came out with a jar of cream which she smoothed onto his wing tips and neck. "This cream is even more potent than the cream I gave you before, it should work quickly."

Favnir almost immediately felt the burning sensation which was still effecting all his body, ease. He felt ready for food. The humans were all eager to hear his story and after they had eaten Favnir told them what had happened. Their faces were rapt and when he told them about the fight with Snydervurm, Puja gasped with horror. Then he told them about his meeting with Nanuk.

"Then there is no more Nanuk?

"That was a terrible experience and I don't want to talk about it in detail. Just say that Nanuk is gone and now there is another Glitter Stone and we left it there under a rock. Elke saved my life."

Favnir suddenly yawned and showed his enormous fangs. Anana noticed his yawn and disappeared inside the tent. She appeared with some blankets which she spread on the snow for the two dragons to use as comfortable bedding. They were soon asleep.

The next three days went quickly and Favnir's wounds healed. Puja never grew tired listening to Favnir's stories over and over again. Favnir was her hero. Elke quietly stood by, not understanding the human language but picking up more and more by listening and watching how they used their bodies.

Now Favnir was looking forward to seeing Carlo again and on the fourth day he was ready to leave. He wondered if Carlo was still happy with Cora and if he wasn't, whether he would want to come back with him to the Sea

Mount. On the whole Favnir didn't think that would be a good idea. Favnir had too much to think of with all his peace making negotiations. He knew Carlo would not have the time or patience for that.

# Chapter Forty-Seven

## Carlo surprises Favnir

Favnir once again said goodbye to his human family and the two dragons left to find Carlo. A few hours' flight and the dragons reached the area where they had left the fox. Now of course there would be a problem. Favnir must find Carlo.

Favnir shouted to Elke. "We will have to fly really slowly and low to the ground. My guess is that they are amongst the trees somewhere." They circled round for ages and saw no sign of Carlo. Favnir was beginning to despair when he caught a glimpse of a quick 'swish' of a magnificent tail in the middle of a small circle of overarching rocks. It was a tail with which he was very familiar. As he flew over Carlo looked up to see why the sun had gone into shadow. When he saw Favnir he yelled with excitement.

"Flash, I've been expecting you for such a long time. I was thinking that something awful had happened. I was just getting ready to come and rescue you, but that might have been a bit difficult at the moment. Come down and you will see. Something wonderful has happened."

*Well, what could that be?* Favnir wondered. He looked at Elke and indicated by a dip of his wing that he would land as close to Carlo as possible. He saw his shadow, dark and clear cut on the snow and drew a deep breath as he landed. Carlo bounded up to him, Favnir saw that he had a new confidence. His tail was even longer and bushier than he remembered and his eyes held a brightness in them that told of contentment.

"Come and see." Carlo led them to the stone circle and proudly waved his paw in the air towards Cora who was lying in a sheltered spot. She was suckling four baby foxes. Cora looked up at Favnir and inclined her head to welcome him but the four cubs continued to suckle.

*How fantastic, Carlo has his own family. I am so happy for him.* Favnir heard his mother's voice as well. *You can let him go now Favnir. Be happy for him and you must not be jealous.*

Aloud he said. "This is wonderful Carlo. If you care for them as you cared for me then you will do a magnificent job."

Carlo skipped around the cubs. They had finished feeding and were trying to walk. Carlo picked one up in his mouth and carried it nearer to Favnir and placed it carefully on the snow. "This is the female, look at her brown patch on her shoulder, just like Cora." He went back and in turn carried each of the tiny cubs over to Favnir. "These are all males, they look like me but one has a tiny brown patch on his shoulder. That one, I am calling him Favnir after you my friend. We haven't decided on the other names. They are only six days old."

Favnir gazed down at his name sake and very carefully touched the tiny cub on his back. He felt water swelling in his eyes. At last Carlo had accepted his name. "This is wonderful Carlo. Thank you for this. I will think of this baby fox every day and I will, of course come back and see him and you and the rest of your family regularly."

Favnir and Elke stayed two days with Carlo and his family but of course Carlo was taken up with providing Cora with food and didn't have much spare time for Favnir. Favnir saw Carlo was happy and on the third day they said goodbye to the foxes and took to the air again. It took all day to reach Sydkap and the sun was setting when they arrived. They spent the night in the same place as before and the following day they departed to fly to Vestaris Seamount. This time Favnir knew the route and the conditions they would meet. As before, the seas were treacherous and the sky was threatening and they landed on the same island to rest. It was a great relief to Favnir when he recognised the flat topped mountain peak appearing on the horizon. *At last my quest has ended and I am home.*

# Chapter Forty-Eight

## Favnir achieves his destiny

Favnir looked over to Elke, as always flying a little bit behind. He knew she was thinking the same as he, that it was so good to be back. She nodded to him and he nodded back.

"Let's go home." She shouted to him and they both made their wings move faster. They raced through the clear blue sky to the island, gradually flying lower as they came closer to landing. Hogruth saw them first. Of late he came out of his cave to look for his son every day peering at the horizon with his failing vision. He stood upright and his heart gave a leap of joy when he saw the two dragons.

Anneka had also seen the dragons. She too looked for them daily and, living outside the cave thought she would be the first one to see their return. As it happened, at the moment when Hogruth had seen them Anneka was looking at the sea. She had seen a family of seals playing in the water and thinking what a nice dinner one of them would make. Movement in the sky made her look up and she saw her friend and Favnir circling round to land.

Favnir landed close to his father and saw that the old dragon was shaking with excitement and joy. Favnir went to him and touched his shoulder and face.

"I'm so glad to be back Father." Hogruth looked at him with a question on his face. "Yes, Snydervurm is dead."

Anneka joined the small group. She rubbed shoulders with Elke and the two went off together into the rocks to talk.

"I'm exhausted Father. Let me rest and eat and later I

will tell you everything. Snydervurm was very compelling and he almost had me in his power."

When Favnir woke hours later he found he was surrounded by a group of dragons. They were waiting for him to wake up so they could hear his story. Elke was nowhere to be seen. He knew she didn't like the cave and was probably even now telling Anneka her side of the story. He rose up to his full height and spoke.

"I will go outside and tell you my story in the open air. That is where it deserves to be told. Don't interrupt me while I'm speaking, you can ask me what you want to know when I have finished."

They followed him out of the cave and he carefully chose the spot where he was on slightly higher ground and the listening dragons were below him. Hogruth sat beside him on the higher level. Favnir stood the whole time so that he could reenact certain parts of the story, especially the fight with Snydervurm. He finished his tale by telling them about his visits to the humans and to Carlo. While Favnir was speaking he noticed Elke and Anneka appearing from between the giant rocks and then joining the group at the back. When Favnir finished his account he motioned to Elke to come forward and stand by him.

"I want to tell you now that this is my partner Elke who will be my guide and advisor in the coming years. We have work to do. The Cohort of Dragons are all dead and we have to gradually introduce ourselves back into human lives. They must know again that we mean well and that we can work together. Once again we can influence them to live peacefully and avoid war about territory and their individual beliefs." There came a roar of approval from the listening dragons and then Hogruth struggled to his feet.

"Favnir is my son and the son of Sedna who is now a

star in the sky. He has shown great courage and initiative. I propose that he becomes co- leader of this group. My last days are approaching and I want to know that I can leave Favnir in charge. He is Favnir Pendragon, Protector of the Weak and Chief of All."

Again the dragons rumbled their approval and Favnir nodded his head in agreement. Favnir then said,

"I will become leader with one condition. I want Elke to be my deputy. She saved my life when we encountered Nanuk and she has proved herself many times."

He heard Sedna's voice. *You have fulfilled your destiny and I am so proud of you. You will no longer hear me, but know I am here by your side and you can look at my star in the sky. Visit Carlo often, he still needs you.*

Favnir did in the end become leader of this group and all the world's dragons. Elke was his partner and deputy. Favnir pursued his dream to lead the peaceful movement to befriend and support humans and he became a legend in his own time.

# Epilogue

In the coming years Favnir's destiny was achieved. He travelled all over the world with Elke and became the leader in the movement which aimed to unite the dragons and humans in peace.

He also regularly visited his human family and saw Puja grow into a beautiful lady who led a group on Earth called 'Make friends with the Dragons'.

Helios and Cidro left the nest in Italy to see the world. They eventually joined the group on Vestaris Seamount and met Anneka again.

Nanuk had disappeared and been transformed into another Glittery Stone. The other Inuit gods continued to be worshipped and feared.

Favnir never, ever forgot his friend Carlo the Arctic Fox and in his visits he watched his namesake grow and become his friend as well. Although he no longer had the stone, he kept Aarja's feather always and treasured it.

Every night when the sky was clear, he looked at his mother Sedna's beautiful star and knew that she was always there by his side.

# Acknowledgements

I would like to thank Blossom Spring Publishing for publishing this book. There are so many people who have given me support but especially I would like to thank my daughter, Suzanne van Leeuwen, who has supplied me with these brilliant illustrations. I would also like to thank Anne Trotman, Hilary Ryan and my son Roger for sub editing. I would especially like to thank Margaret Jennings who read the first and second drafts and offered many valuable suggestions. I feel I must include my writing group, the Springwood Writers who have always given me friendly advice. I want to thank Charlotte Comley who gave me much needed encouragement in the early stages of the book. I especially want to thank a close friend who has supported me from start to finish and given me back my self-belief.

# About The Author

Jeni Joyce is the pseudonym for a writer of fantasy. She writes both long and short stories for children and adults. Jeni was educated at Leicester and Winchester Universities with a degree in Botany and an M.A. in Archaeology.

Her work has been highly commended by a Write Time short story competition. Publication includes poetry for United Press and short stories for the local press and online for the Nonsuch Dulcimer Club.

Jeni was born in Great Yarmouth and now lives in Hampshire near family and friends. She spends her leisure time swimming, walking, playing bridge, reading and keeping up to date with Archaeology.

She is a member of The Springfield Writers group.

www.blossomspringpublishing.com

Printed in Great Britain
by Amazon